GW01372822

Ghosts at Cock Crow
The Story of Failand

Rita Archer

REDCLIFFE
Bristol

First published in 1987
by Redcliffe Press Ltd.,
49 Park St., Bristol.

© Rita Archer

ISBN 0 948265 12 4

To the memory of Dorothy Cooke, who loved Failand.

All rights reserved. No part of this publication may be reproduced, stored in a retrieval system, or transmitted, in any form or by any means, electronic, mechanical, photocopying, recording or otherwise, without the prior permission of the publishers.

Photoset, printed and bound by
WBC Bristol and Maesteg

Contents

Introduction	7
The Riddle of the Wansdyke	9
The naming of Failand	14
The House of Berkeley	18
Maurice and Isabel	24
The de Faylands	28
'A considerable village'	30
Failand and the Picturesque	35
Two schools	40
The Frys of Failand	45
Chapel and Church	65
Failand School in the Twentieth Century	69
The other house	72
The market gardeners	75
The Flora of Failand	79
Failand in Wartime (1939-44)	81
End Piece	84
Books consulted	86

Acknowledgements

I am grateful to Miss Frances Poole for allowing me to include her reminiscences of Failand School, to Elisabeth Robinson for her sketch of Failand House, and to all those who lent me photographs and other memorabilia. My thanks are due also to all the Failand people who searched their memories on my behalf. Finally, I am particularly indebted to the late Mrs. Lucy Bowden whose little books on Failand have proved invaluable in putting together the story of our hamlet.

"The poetry of history lies in the quasi-miraculous fact that once on this familiar spot of ground walked other men and women, actual as we are today, thinking their own thoughts, swayed by their own passions, but now all gone, one generation vanishing into another, gone as utterly as we ourselves shall shortly be gone, like ghosts at cockcrow."

    G.M. Trevelyan *Autobiography of a historian.*

"The dancers are all gone under the hill."

    T.S. Eliot.

Introduction

However striking a piece of historical information may be, under certain circumstances it refuses to come alive. I read once that "in 1286 the heir to the Earl of Warenne was killed in a tournament at Croydon". That somehow incongruous fact stirred nothing in my imagination; it remained dead and buried beneath the concrete and tarmac of modern urban development.

A quite opposite difficulty is presented in a place which we know holds the secrets of a rich past but which is now only empty countryside; the evidence is gone as surely as if the ground had disappeared beneath a modern city, and the history must be drawn up from under the green fields. This is the situation in Failand, the little hamlet in which I live. Perhaps the absence of evidence here is a part of the reason why I have done nothing till now, nearly twenty years after coming to the place to live, to uncover the story of my home ground. The other reason is less easy to explain. There is I think at a certain stage in life an active preference to live in the present, even a positive disinclination to probe into the past. Then, for no reason other than that the time is right, comes the urge to reach out and touch the lives of the people who have lived where you live now. This was the moment when I began to pay attention to my immediate surroundings and listen to the tales my friends and neighbours had to tell. And so I have written what follows, studies of the distant and more immediate past of the hamlet of Failand.

At first sight this is an insignificant place. A 19th century local historian speaks of it as "an outlying hamlet of the parish of Wraxall . . . curiously intermixed with a similar section of the adjoining parish of Portbury". During most of their history all three places were in the county of Somerset; the abomination of the up-to-date name Avon we can safely ignore. The Clifton Suspension Bridge and the City of Bristol are only some five miles away, but apart from a modern development confined within 60 acres at its edge, Failand consists of only a few scattered houses and farms set among woods and fields.

For all its nearness to Bristol it feels remote and very old and it has always held a fascination for those who really know it. Many mysteries surround it. There is the mystery of the very name of the place, which etymologists have tried in vain to explain; the mystery of the Wansdyke in its midst, that great fortification of the Dark Ages whose origin and purpose have always remained an enigma, and which in Failand is turned seaward against some enemy from the West; and the mystery which has driven at least one local historian almost to distraction in her efforts to solve it, the presence here at one time of a considerable village now entirely lost but for a single stone buttress and the echo of a tale of a name upon an old gatepost.

You may add this final poser. What became of a mighty mansion, the second principal standing house of the noble family of Berkeley, which once stood up on Windmill Hill just beyond the border of Failand with Portbury? One astonished gentleman noted in the 19th century that "had the earth swallowed it up it could not have disappeared more completely."

The other source of particular interest in Failand is the domination of the tiny hamlet for nearly three quarters of a century by a unique family, the Frys; not the 'chocolate' Frys, although closely related to them, but the family of a distinguished judge, Sir Edward Fry, who came with his beautiful wife Mariabella and his large family to live at Failand House at the end of the nineteenth century. One son was Roger, the brilliant art critic and considerable artist, and friend of Virginia Woolf, who wrote his biography. One daughter was Margery, Principal of Somerville College, Oxford, penal reformer, and friend of many great men and women. The other children, all of whom lived in Failand at some time in their lives, were also interesting and distinctive personalities. The story of this family is told in some depth for there are local memories of them in plenty to draw upon. There is much to tell, too, of the lives of ordinary men in these later years of Failand's history, and of one not so ordinary. The famous cricketer W.G. Grace was educated at the private school which flourished in upper Failand during the nineteenth century.

My own training is not in history; it is a literary one. My advantage in what I have tried to do has been many years lived in the hamlet with time to notice the small things which a stranger might pass by, time enough to know and talk to the real Failand people, time enough to catch the gleam of the place.

The riddle of the Wansdyke

There is a field on the borders of Portbury and Lower Failand called by local people Humpy Ground. You can see how it got its name if you stand on the rising land above it and look across to the bottom end. Down there is a medley of mounds and ditches, and behind, at a lower level, a flat platform, its edge outlined by a symmetrical curve. In the next field there are more similar humps and bumps. This second field runs alongside the lane which leads down to Portbury village. When you come out into the lane by the field gate you find yourself opposite a stile which leads into a broad, deep gully. The gully runs up between two high banks, through Oakham Spinney and out on to the slopes of Windmill Hill.

What you are seeing, in these fields and woodland ways, are the last faint lineaments in our neighbourhood of a great fortification which may have been already old by the time the Saxon invaders of Britain came upon it. With its huge mounds and ditches it must be, they thought, the work of a supernatural creature, and where they met it as they moved across the South of England they named it after their great Norse god Woden, Woden's Dyke, or Wans Dyke. How it got there was a mystery to them, and something of a mystery it has remained to this day. Yet here a part of it unmistakably is, in Lower Failand, in Mr. Fennel's cowpasture.

Once your eye has picked up traces of the dyke it is easy to be persuaded that you can see it everywhere. What you thought must be the last vestiges of an earthen wall proves, however, to be the line of a hedge, grubbed out only a few years before and quickly overgrown by grass. There is a hedgerow of young holly and ash saplings running across the sloping meadow opposite the front of Stone Cottage which grows upon a raised bank; if you poke about you find that this bank is full of stones, the ancient core, you might think, of a turf wall, now shrunk almost to nothing. Or were the stones simply thrown up the top end of the field by a farmer as he cleared the ground? That could be the explanation. Yet there are other things, not so easily explained away. If you go back to Humpy Ground you can find and follow a pretty well-defined ditch, which runs right through the bottom of Sandy Lane. In a field below the village school you can pick out the lines of what must have been an artificially constructed bank, which disappears into a small spinney at the top of the same lane. Across by Lower Failand Farm, if you follow the little road down the short hill towards Abbots Leigh, you find that it keeps close under a surprisingly high bank which is loosely compacted in parts, and always liable to landslip in wet weather. At the bottom of this hill, standing like a buttress against a ramification of the bank, is Laurel Farm; the steep back garden here occasionally collapses into the yard.

The impression is strong all the way down the hill of a road built along the line of an old man-made boundary. Go back up the hill to Lower Failand Farm, and this time walk past the front door towards Ham Green. In the fields on the right are more earthworks like the ones already seen in the valley bottom. If you follow the little lane towards Ham Green it climbs and turns westward until you find yourself on the crest of an escarpment, which although it is a natural feature rises here almost as if it were intended to assist anyone trying to defend the surrounding countryside. This scarp is so steep to the south as to be unassailable, and to the north it commands unimpeded views to the mouth of the Avon and the sea.

What we need now is an expert to interpret our random observation, and by the greatest good fortune that is what we have. A well-known west-country archaeologist walked through our lanes and fields sometime in the nineteen twenties and charted what he believed to be the complete series of fortifications in the Failand valley. His name was Albany Major and he put down his findings in a chapter which he contributed to a book called *The Mystery of the Wansdyke*. Dealing with the section of the dyke which runs through North Somerset he begins on the mudflats near Portbury; all the historians seem to agree that the western end of Wansdyke runs out into the Bristol Channel at this point. He traces it back through Portbury village and across the fields east of Oakham Farm, bringing it into Failand through the broad gully which we already know, by the stile in Oakham Spinney. "From this point there appear to be at least three lines of the dyke traceable, the two rearmost keeping to the high ground, the third running through the Lower Failand valley". This third, or front line, is the one from Humpy Ground which follows the ditch to The Dell, at the bottom of Sandy Lane. Of the two higher lines one, the lower of the two, follows roughly "the line of hedgerows along the slope of the hill below the parish boundary, till it approaches Jubbes Court when it crosses the road (i.e. the lane to Portbury) and beyond the house (Jubbes Court) can be traced across a field below the schools". This description covers the raised hedgebank in the field seen from the Stone Cottage front windows, and the just discernible lines of the bank below the school. The highest line of the dyke runs up on the downland alongside the boundary between Wraxall and Failand and turns across past school, church and Failand House, following the line of the present road. These two higher lines meet somewhere by Lower Failand Farm, and Mr. Major links them to the defence in the valley bottom by bringing this lowest line up from the Dell through the rising fields to the earthworks behind the farmhouse.

From this point the dyke goes in two directions. Mr. Major maps its main course as following the Abbots Leigh road down past — or rather through — Laurel Farm, as we have guessed, and away through Long Ashton to Dundry and so on its way eastward towards Devizes. The particular defensive work of our valley is completed to the westward, "formed by a scarp sloping upwards and rising steeply from the valley, its northern face commands a clear view over ground that slopes down very gradually to the river in the far distance . . . Westwards the line is continued along the lane to Jubbes Wood . . . There is nothing to show how it ended . . . It has all the appearance of an outpost line thrown forward to the top of the slope north of the valley, to enable a watch to be kept to the north towards the sea and mouth of the Avon". All this backs up our own impression of the scarp as a natural feature incorporated into the defensive scheme of the valley.

What we have in Failand then is a complicated set of earthworks turned seawards. Whatever the function of Wansdyke elsewhere it looks here like a series of obstacles put up against plunderers coming in from the western sea. What we now need to try to find out is when the fortifications were constructed. Here the archaeologists are not so helpful. Mr. Major and his fellow members of the Somerset Archaeological Society were plainly fascinated by the problem. In the Society's papers for 1924 there is an account of a meeting on Wansdyke at Pensford. Unfortunately, Albany Major himself, for some reason, could not be there and as an acknowledged expert on the dyke he was obviously missed. Mr. St. George Gray, himself well-known for his pre-historic excavations, "explained with regret that Mr. A. Major was unable to be present. We had in that position (in Pensford) a vallum and fosse very clearly defined of much larger dimensions than most of the Wansdyke in Somerset. It was here he (Mr. Major or Mr. Gray? — it is not clear) had hoped to make a sectional cutting in time for the visit of the Society, but it had been impossible, owing to the lateness of the season, and the grass, intended for hay, was still standing". At Pensford, as in Failand, the great earthworks had been absorbed over the centuries into the agricultural life of the district. "No excavations — except a few on a small scale — had taken place across Wansdyke since the end of the last century, when General Pitt-Rivers[1] made some systematic cuttings in the neighbourhood of Devizes. In that part of Wiltshire the dyke proved to be Roman, Romano-British, or Post Roman". The General gives us here a wide option as to dates, and it is possible to deduce from this that different sections may have been built at different times.

The consensus of expert opinion seems to be that the main part of

---

[1] a distinguished archaeologist.

Wansdyke, that between Devizes and Bath, was erected in the second part of the fifth century, and was the work of Ambrosius Aurelianus, a Romano-British tribal chief; he was one of a number who took control after the departure of the Romans in the early part of that century, and who tried to organize some kind of defence against the lawless forces threatening Britain within and without. If the dyke were built after the Romans had gone it must certainly have been the work of someone bred in the Roman tradition, who had their capacity to plan and complete such a vast undertaking. Along its principal section the ditch is always on the northward side of the structure, facing any enemy coming from that direction. This would be effective against the Picts, who, once Roman discipline had disintegrated, foraged far south of Hadrian's Wall, almost the whole length of England. It would also act as a barrier against the Anglo Saxon tribes brought in by the British in the mid-fifth century to help repel the Picts, and who themselves turned invaders, gaining a foothold in the South East and gradually moving westwards.

None of this, however, explains our own section of the dyke. Who was the enemy to the westward, across the sea? From the mid-fourth century onwards, well before the eventual departure of the Romans to defend their crumbling empire in Europe, the whole western side of our island lived in fear of the Irish. One historian[2] tells us: "On its western flank, Britain from Argyll to Cornwall lay open to the Irish, whose curraghs could ferry slave raiders and booty hunters over numerous short sea crossings", and another[3]: "At the beginning of the fifth century we are in what may be called the classical period of Irish piracy. Niall of the Nine Hostages, High King of Ireland from A.D. 389 to 405, is the greatest figure . . . He met his death in a raid at sea off the Isle of Wight, doubtless at the hands of a Romano-British coastal patrol."

In our own immediate area a folk tale recorded by the local historian, Gray Usher, tells how the people of Clevedon would flee for shelter to the old Iron Age Camp at Cadbury, because 'the Red Men' were coming, no doubt the red-headed pirates from Ireland. There have been a great many finds of buried coins in North Somerset, of dates which suggest they were hidden during these last years of Roman occupation. One was at Tickenham, and contained money dated A.D. 260–373. A paper written in 1927 for the Somerset Archaeological Society records that this hoard, uncovered about a foot below the surface, "had presumably been buried in a wooden receptacle bound with iron, fragments of both substances being found on the spot. Pieces of skin bore the impressions of coins, which was evidence that the money had been wrapped in that material. The whole

---

[2] Charles Thomas: *Britain & Ireland in Early Christian Times*
[3] Collingwood & Myers. *Roman Britain & the English Settlements*

stood upon two flat pieces of sandstone, and a cover may have been formed by a shallow earthenware dish, the fragments of which were also found. Adjoining the site was a rough stone floor, on and around which were the bones of animals, spindle whorls, and pottery shards."

The owners who so carefully buried their wealth plainly hoped to come back and recover it, but were ominously prevented. Elsewhere in Somerset stores of coins have turned up in pottery urns, their mouths stopped with a pebble to keep the contents from spilling. One hoard was simply wrapped in a handful of grass and wedged between two stones. On the evidence of these hidden monies people hereabouts would certainly seem to have been frightened and insecure.

By all accounts the threat from Ireland diminished steadily from the beginning of the fifth century onwards, after the death of Niall the High King. Our particular piece of defensive work would certainly have been needed long before the second half of the century. By that time Ambrosius Aurelianus' chief concern was probably to protect with his fortification the whole of his kingdom in the South West from a variety of threats, but chiefly from the Picts and the Saxons. He rested the eastern end of his great dyke on the edge of the impenetrable forests which in those days formed a protective cover all the way down to Southampton Water. Perhaps he rested the western end here, on our set of defensive works already in existence against the incursions from Ireland since the last years of the Roman occupation.

It is all guesswork. These were the Dark Ages and dark they remain. It does us good after dealing in 'ifs' and 'perhaps' to come back at the end to where we began, among the grassy mounds and ditches of Humpy Ground. Here, at some time between the last years of Roman occupation and the first coming of the Saxons into the South West of Britain, was the focus of a serious attempt to defend the Somerset coast against invaders from across the sea. The dates are obscure, the great earthen walls, the deep ditches and enclosures almost obliterated, but the great winds moan and blow from the South West still, as they always did, and mists hide the valley bottoms from the keenest eye. The conditions for anxious watch are quite unchanged and we can feel with the watchers. We have a real piece of history in our midst.

The naming of Failand

Beside the site of the Roman Temple which came to light when the new school was being built at Portbury lay a Saxon cemetery. Here the archaeologists found a collection of human bones shovelled higgledy piggledy into the ground without benefit of decent burial. A quick tidying up job seems to have been done, after a pitched battle. There would almost certainly have been some fierce fighting when the Saxons first reached Portbury, not least because the Romano-British in the neighbourhood would be directly descended from those who had manned the Wansdyke against invasion generations before. Glastonbury had fallen to the Saxons in A.D. 640 and by the early eighth century Congresbury was in their hands. At some time in the same century they must have reached our locality, not from the North East — perhaps the old line of the Dyke still held there — but from the South. Like all the Germanic people they preferred to live on flat ground with plenty of running water, and so when the fighting was done they chose to settle on the low land, building their fortification or burh near river and estuary. The waters of the Bristol Channel in those days lapped against the land immediately beyond where the present village of Portbury stands. The name explains itself: Port-byrig[1], the port at the fortification.

What these new settlers found when they ventured up the valley into the higher ground at the back of their dwellings must have been a great puzzle to them. The whole place would have been straddled by the still undiminished mounds of the Wansdyke, and further up, somewhere near what is now Summerhouse Wood, stood great boulders, probably in some kind of formal arrangement, placed there by the Bronze Age peoples some fifteen hundred years before. Field names are the most trustworthy clues to the history of the neighbourhood and the field by Summerhouse has always been known locally as Hengaston. Turn this word on end and you get ston henga, the hanging stones, the same name which the Saxons gave to the huge standing stones on Salisbury Plain. Perhaps the invaders saw these first up there looming through the mist, so that they seemed to hang as if by magic from the transverse stones which completed the arches. The Portbury

---

[1] 'byrig' is the OE dative form of 'burh'.

Saxons must have given their cromlech the same descriptive name, though probably by now its imaginative origin was forgotten[2].

As they pushed on even further into the hills the villagers would have come on another such strange sight. We know from the Rev. Masters' 19th century *History of Wraxall* that within the memory of some he knew, a "cromlech of prehistoric antiquity" stood to the west of what is now Failand Lodge farm, "the destruction of which is much to be deplored". In addition to all the mysterious relics of a past he could not envisage, unexplained mounds and ditches, circles of mighty stones, the Saxon would be bound to have caught sight of something which he would connect at once with the supernatural world — all over the high downland he would have found the worked flint arrowheads of the Stone Age people. In folklore it was commonly related that the flint arrowhead was the weapon of a supernatural creature, the Saxon name for which was oelf, or in its later form elf. This weapon was called an elf shot or elf arrow. The elf in Northern tales, the tales the Saxons knew, was usually a creature of evil disposition and fearsome appearance, ugly and mis-shapen, with long arms and matted unkempt hair, elf-locks. Full of mischief and malevolence, he would fire his arrows at men or their cattle so that they sickened and died. Not long ago, a farmer's wife hereabouts showed me an old cigar box crammed full of beautiful specimens of flint tools and weapons, collected on her husband's land over a period of some forty years, whenever the plough threw them up. (Some others were found in the garden of Stone Cottage by the Curator of the Bristol Museum, Hans Schubart, who lived there for many years). How thankfully the superstitious Saxons of Portbury must have fled such horrid finds and scurried back down to their settlement below.

Now no-one seems to know how Failand got its name. One local historian, Mrs. Lucy Bowden, suggested that it derived from the Saxon word, feoh, meaning property or land, and that it referred to the way in which the land was held in Saxon times. Sir Edward Fry, a great lover of Failand, who lived here a hundred years ago, and whose story comes later in these pages, tried hard to solve the mystery. According to Agnes, his daughter, it had always been "a standing etymological puzzle", and no doubt he and his clever family gave the subject a thorough academic airing. Although they probably discounted the simple explanation often heard in the district, that Failand is simply short for Fairyland, the Rev. Masters in his *History of Wraxall* mentions it in passing. "Failand's . . . exceptional beauty of situation may lend colour to (this) tradition". Local opinion in

---

[2] Hengaston is a common field name in Somerset, no doubt to mark the presence once of a prehistoric monument. In Yatton the form is corrupted to Hangstone; another version found is Hangasson. Our own field is sometimes called this.

such matters is always worth paying attention to and we should bear it in mind as we struggle for the answer.

By and large it must be admitted that the Saxons named their towns and settlements in prosaic fashion: Wealh-ton (Walton) the settlement of the Welsh, Clappa's ton (Clapton) the settlement belonging to Clappa. Yet they were not without imagination in the bestowing of names; they aptly and beautifully named the Hanging Stones. Why should they not then name the high wild place behind their homes, haunted as it seemed to be by strange and fearsome things, Oelfland. In their folk tales the Elves were believed to dwell in chambered mounds, and the Saxons had certainly seen such places up there[3], and had seen too the elf arrows lying on the bare downland. And when the Normans came, the new conquerers, bringing their own language with them, they had their own French word for a supernatural creature, fae[4]. Faeland would slip a great deal more easily off their tongues than the gutteral oelfland. Other spellings of the name, found in the middle ages were Foeland and Foiland, and it is tempting to imagine that here we have an English compromise, the f in the old form, Oelfland, transposed to produce an amalgam of the Saxon and Norman word.

Perhaps the local tradition which links the name of the hamlet with enchantment and magic, with faery, is not so far adrift. Even as late as the beginning of the 20th century the upper parts of Failand suggested to the people who lived there not the prettified setting for the popular image of the fairy but something much more frightening. The upper road running from Clevedon to Bristol, now an urbanised highway to take commuters to and from the city was certainly in winter a wild and frightening place seventy or eighty years back, before the new houses began to appear on the Sixty Acre development. Plenty of Failand people have heard as much from their mothers and fathers. Some years ago a poem appeared in the Failand Church Magazine. It was called simply "Failand Road". The author was a Mr. Reginald Hopes; the verse is not expert but there is no mistaking the strength of feeling which produced it:

> The top road over Failand
> Is the weirdest road I know.
> When Autumn leaves are falling
> Alone I dare not go
> A-riding o'er the top road
> With its eerie, misty land,
> And the whisp'ring and the shuddering
> Of the trees on either hand.
> . . . . . .

---

[3] the ruins of Wansdyke.
[4] old French.

I've seen 'mong purpling tree-tops
The witches brooms a-flying,
And loud above the owl
I've heard lost children crying:
And something's rushed behind me
Straining hard to clutch my hair
And though I dared not look behind
I always felt it there,
Till my breath has almost left me
As I've rushed the whole way down,
Never stopping never turning
Till the lights of Bristol town
Have clustered round to cheer me:
And now I dare not go
O'er the top road over Failand —
T'is the weirdest road I know.

The Portbury Saxons would certainly have understood.

The House of Berkeley

As the traveller from Portbury reaches the border with Failand, he enters a deeply cut stretch of the lane, full of foxgloves and hart's tongue fern and over-arched with trees, some of them sizeable oaks. The dark trunks of these old trees thrust out precariously above the top of the steep banks, held fast by a mass of exposed roots. Coming up out of this green tunnel into the broad day one is confronted almost at once by high open downland ahead and rising sharply on the right. These smooth slopes look ideal for the exercising of horses, and nowadays thoroughbreds from a nearby racing stable can often be seen prancing delicately in the lower fields before moving at full gallop across the higher ground, and streaming out a few seconds later against the skyline.

Many hundreds of years ago Failand people must have stood a few minutes to watch and admire, just as we do, the brave sight of great handsome horses being ridden up there on the hillside, for in the Middle Ages the high lands in Portbury and Failand were alive with horsemen. They rode out principally from the mansion of the Berkeley family on Windmill Hill at the back of Portbury village. That family's steward in Elizabethan times, John Smyth, wrote down their history, and he tells us how the young men of the household used to train on the downs by the great house "in all martiall exercises, running with launces, hastilitudes, spearplay and the like". Unbelievable as it now seems, on our own green hills above the Failand valley once rode a young knight who, having learnt his craft on Portbury Down, attended the Black Prince himself, fighting beside him at Crécy. This young man was Maurice Berkeley, brought up, as were most of the Berkeley heirs, in the house on Windmill Hill. At the age of eight his father had taken him campaigning in Scotland, at fourteen he was in the train of the Black Prince in Spain and France, and eventually, in 1356 he was taken prisoner by the French at Poitiers. Not only men training in the arts of war but hunting parties, out looking for sport and meat, covered the hills and rode through the wooded valleys below. The Berkeley house, second only in importance for the family to their castle in Gloucestershire, is still spoken of locally as the Hunting Lodge; in its heyday however it was a good deal more than that.

To find out how the Berkeley family came to live in Portbury and build one of their 'principal standing houses' on Windmill Hill, to cast its powerful shadow over all the neighbourhood, we must look back to Saxon times. Then the great Godwin family owned Portbury among its many holdings in Somerset. (Harold, defeated at Hastings, was a Godwin) If members of this family visited their lands hereabouts they would have stayed in Portbury itself, an important Saxon settlement, their lodging probably a simple wooden hall. Soon after the coming of the Normans the Portbury Hundred[1] came into the possession of a wealthy Bristol merchant and lawyer, Robert Fitzhardinge. His grandfather, a Saxon called Ealnoth, had served both the Saxon King Edward the Confessor and later William the Norman Conqueror. Robert, like Ealnoth, served the Norman monarchy well, and was rewarded not only with the gift of the Portbury Hundred, but also the hundreds of Bedminster and Hartcliff, and eventually the gift of the Honour of Berkeley; an Honour was a collection of manors. Berkeley, in Gloucestershire, gave the Fitzhardinge family their new name. As the family grew in importance the old hall at Portbury, built in Saxon days, was no doubt improved, but the chief preoccupation would have been with the construction of a castle at Berkeley. The building of the second 'principal standing house', the new manor at Portbury, was not carried out until the end of the thirteenth century.

Thomas Berkeley the Second, in whose time the second family house was built, needed plenty of room; his "household and standing domestical family was two hundred persons and upward, knights, esquires, yeoman, grooms and pages, besides husbandmen, hindes and such of lower condition". It has astounded local historians that nothing is now left of such an important dwelling place, "Had the earth swallowed it up it could not have disappeared more completely", wrote 'WJR' in his short history of Portbury, and Eve Wigan, in 'Tales of Gordano', tells us that up on Windmill Hill only a few heaps of undressed stone remain to mark where it stood. Those who know the neighbourhood better have seen more than this. On the hill, hidden deep in the larch plantations which now cover most of it, is a considerable length of wall, outlining a rectangular area quite large enough to contain the magnificence of the Berkeley domain. In most places this wall has collapsed but a few lengths still stand, the cornerstones properly shaped for the purpose. Other walls or mounds of stone mark off enclosures standing against the main outline, and the remains of walled ways run off in the direction of abundant springs which now feed a reservoir, springs which would easily have met the large demands of a noble household, 'WJR', he who marvelled at the complete disappearance of the mansion, writes a little later in his book that "a Mr. Snook, who died some years ago, remembered seeing part of the foundations and a huge chimney, which when pulled down supplied

---

[1] hundred: a subdivision of a county.

sufficient material for some of the farm buildings"; he here refers to Honor Farm on the border of Portbury and Failand below Windmill Hill which still stands. We can guess from the date of WJR's booklet that Mr. Snook's memory probably stretched back to the early part of the nineteenth century. There is no doubt that farmers and others in the locality must have helped themselves liberally to the excellent stone standing there for the taking. It was (and is) common country practice[2] and goes far to explain how large solid constructions can disappear without trace. We know that by the late eighteenth century the great mediaeval building had finally fallen into decay. A windmill (which must have given the hill its name) is marked on a map of 1782 as standing on the hilltop and the huge ruts of the carts which carried the grain up from the surrounding countryside are still distinctly to be seen. An empty cart returning down the hill to Portbury could easily bring along a load of good stone. Such regular traffic would make short work of dismantling the house.

The most interesting relic of the Berkeley occupation familiar to local people but unaccountably neglected by local historians (except Mrs. Lucy Bowden who notes its existence) is still to be found at the entrance to Oakham Spinney, at the very point where the lane from Portbury runs up out of the over-arching tunnel of trees described earlier in the chapter. There, almost hidden among brambles and ivy, are the remains of a considerable tower. A close look at the ruin on the side that faces the lane, reveals a number of small apertures spaced at regular intervals; these are putlog holes, left in the wall by the mediaeval masons for the insertion of the scaffolding needed for repair work. At the base of the tower is what appears to be a large drainage hole, squared off with a beautiful regular slab of local red sandstone.

The tower stands at the bottom of a gulley, which runs up between two high banks marking the course of the Wansdyke as it crosses into Failand. This convenient way up to the hilltop, protected by the remains of that ancient fortification, was ideal for what was probably one of the main approaches to the Berkeley mansion; the tower at the foot would secure it against attack. One of the names in the list of taxpayers in the Portbury Hundred in 1327 is Wilelmo atte Torre. Torre is a likely form of the word tower in the days when spelling was an individual matter, so perhaps

---

[2] As illustrated in the *Proceedings for 1928 of the Somerset Archaeological Society*.
"excavations at Claverton: The Manor House at Claverton . . . had two predecessors. It was known that the first stood in a field called Orchard Close, south of the church. It was built . . . circa 1340, but no vestige of it remains today, except some banks and heaps, which are said to mark the site . . . the banks seem to enclose space 70 feet in length by 66 feet in width. Towards the centre of this space a very rough stone floor was uncovered, which may have been merely the broken pieces left behind when the best was taken. All walls down to the lowest foundations appear to have been removed, the rubbish only being left behind. It is said that the Tudor House, Bassett Farm, opposite the site, was built entirely with stone taken from this old manor".

William was custodian of the gatehouse at that time. The heavy traffic of horsemen, carts and foot passengers up to the house may well have been responsible for cutting the lane so deeply down into the soft red earth where it leads from the tower towards Portbury.

All these reasonable assumptions about the position and size of the Berkeley house itself and the nature of the approach to it are wonderfully verified by the 1830 Ordnance Survey map, the first edition, which has recently been made generally available. The cartographer saw and marked off a large rectangular area on the summit of Windmill Hill, most clearly shown as approached by an unbroken driveway curving up from the tower. Another well defined wide path is shown running in a straight line from the mansion down to Honor Farm. Mr. Snook may well have seen the materials for the farm buildings brought down this very way.

The great attraction of the Portbury house to the Berkeley family must always have been the riding. Even in Saxon times the downland had been used for horsebreeding. Domesday Book records an unusually high number of "wild mares" in Portbury. The Bishop of Coutances, the 'fighting bishop', a favourite of the Conqueror, was given Portbury Hundred as part of an immediate gift after the Norman victory at Hastings in 1066. He is reported to have had one hundred and thirty mares in the neighbourhood, sixty of which he kept at Long Ashton, and the rest, one guesses, on Portbury Downs.

Among our old field and place names which are the best guide we have to our distant past there are a number connected with horses. One large flat expanse high on the Downs is called The Horse Race and there is a Racecourse Farm nearby (the home today of a large racing stable). Local tradition says it was the Romans who first raced their horses up here. The land behind New Farm, in the same immediate area, is called The Paddock. 'Paddock' is from the Saxon 'pearroc'; perhaps this was one of the enclosures where the Bishop of Coutances or the Saxons before him, kept their breeding mares.

The heirs to the Berkeley title, brought up by custom in the lesser family property at Portbury, all learnt to ride on the downs. Thomas Berkeley the Second, he who had built the new manor house, had three sons. To one of them, John, his father gave when he was eight years old "a hors which cost 5 shillings, when he began to ride upon the downes of Portbury". Another son, Maurice, grew up to be the son who "frequented the downes in all martiall exercises". He jousted all over England including Kenilworth, where his grandfather before him had been killed in a tournament. Maurice's grandson it was who fought at Crécy beside the Black Prince.

The high downs, so suitable for riding, were probably clear of all but a few trees. The Berkeley estate however had at least two enclosed wooded areas. A reference is made in 1514 to the appointment of a Royal Bailiff to the Lordship of Portbury; the estate had at this much later date reverted for a time to the Crown. This bailiff was in charge of "the herbage and pannage of the hyer and nether park therein, and the 3 gardens called le gret and lytell Conygar". Herbage is the right to pasture but pannage refers to the right of pasturing swine in woodland. The wooded parks probably dated from the early Middle Ages, when it was the practice to make enclosures to prevent deer from straying, preserving them handily for the huntsmen whenever meat (or sport) was needed. The higher park would have been somewhere near the Horse Race — there is a farm there still called Higher Farm. The lower or nether park was probably in the immediate neighbourhood of the house. A few stout oaks and the name Oakham Spinney suggest it was once heavily wooded there. (The huge ash trees in the area are perhaps descended from those which provided the very best wood to make lances for jousting.) The other responsibility of the Royal Bailiff, "three gardens called le gret and lytell Conygar", must have been upon the warm and gentle slopes of Conygar Hill and its companion grassy mound down in Portbury, providing the produce for the kitchens of the mansion on the more exposed ground above the village.

It was during the lifetime of Thomas the Rich, Baron of Berkeley from 1326–1361, that the Portbury manor house was at its most prosperous. This noble lord, returning to his estates after a period of imprisonment, set about putting them in tip-top order. While he was absent all his "manorhouses, granges, stables, oxhouses, mills, waynes, carts and plows had become much decayed. He frequented himself at all the great fairs at Wells, Gloucester and Tetbury, to buy fresh cattle and grain"[3]. He would have re-stocked the Berkeley Castle estate from the fairs at Gloucester and Tetbury; Wells would be much more convenient for the Portbury lands. The ox was the draught animal which pulled the plough in the Middle Ages, sometimes as many as eight oxen to one plough.

Oxhouse Lane is still the name of the narrow road running between Upper and Lower Failand, and in the dip, on the right hand side going towards Portbury, are a handful of ruined walls, facing immediately upon the lane. In the hollow a little way into the wood (the trunk of an ancient and long dead oak is hidden there among much younger trees) are further small remains of walling, perhaps the partitions of a large stable. The old local names prove so reliable hereabouts that this place is almost certainly the sight of the Berkeley oxhouses. A rich sheltered vale stretches back from it up towards Failand Farm, ideal grazing for beasts. Smyth tells us that even in the 16th century this was still known as Ox Croft — "some say the grounds are noe worth, but lately they have become good pasture and

---

[3] John Smyth: *Lives of the Berkeleys.*

meadow". The method of ploughing in the Middle Ages left high ridges or 'balks' between the furrows, and in one of the fields of Lower Failand Farm it is still possible to pick out some of these, perhaps the last traces of the arable land worked by the peasants and held by them in return for services to the Lords of the Manor, here almost certainly the Berkeleys. Each family would hold one or more narrow strips of ground called a land, and this ancient term is still retained in the field name; the Lower Failand Farm field is called "the small lands". There are other fields in the same area bearing similar names: Longlands in Portbury, Sidelands, corrupted to Sidling, in Failand.

Just over the boundary of Failand, in Easton-in-Gordano, not very far from the ploughlands, is a small open space called the Common, reached from Failand along Common Lane. Here the peasants in the Middle Ages would have had the right to pasture their animals, a right which was still exercised in the early nineteenth century. A Failand resident was told by her aged mother, who heard it from *her* grandfather, that when great-grandmother was a little girl she remembered seeing all kinds of animals grazing up there. It is also remembered that just below the Common lay Glebe land, the property of Easton Church, and there are still some who can recall that this was cultivated to raise produce for the needy poor of Easton as late as the nineteen twenties.

Apart from the common lands which lay up on the high hills, Failand, in the Middle Ages, would seem to have owed its character almost entirely to its being part of the estate of a noble family; parkland, downland, arable land, stabling for oxen and other cattle, and all under the lord's domain. Yet the hamlet lay conveniently close to Bristol, its air sweet after the smells of a great city. If the Berkeleys could be persuaded to sell a piece of their land then a wealthy merchant might build himself a fair house in the country and move in and out of town with relative ease. One such family is at the centre of our next chapter.

Maurice and Isabel

Perhaps the most fascinating story from Failand's distant past concerns a family quarrel. The two families involved were the Berkeleys and the Medes of Medes Place in Failand, and the bad feeling arose when Maurice, the heir to the Berkeley title, fell in love with Isabel, daughter of Philip Mede, a merchant, and his wife Isabel. Terrible trouble followed, as it often does when people of very different backgrounds decide to marry.

The Mede family was a well known one in Bristol in the Middle Ages. Philip Mede's father had been Sheriff of Bristol. Philip was three times mayor in the 1450's and 60's, and the Medes were described as "wealthy merchants and citizens of Bristol in the Parish of St Mary Redcliffe". No doubt as well as their country place in Failand they had a town house and business premises in Bristol. There is an elaborate set of tombs in St. Mary's, called the Mede Chantry, probably put there by Philip so that mass could be sung in it for the repose of his own soul, when the time came, and for the souls of his family. Philip and his wife were buried there; on one of the tombs their stylized figures, conventionally carved in stone, lie side by side. Philip wears the sober gown and mantle of a wealthy merchant, with a leathern bag at the waist, the badge of his calling. Isabel, plainly dressed perhaps because the stonemason could not manage elaborate trimmings, has a high, 'pedimental' head-dress with veils hanging from its point.

Local tradition has it that the family's Failand house stood just above the valley where Failand Hill House stands today. One possibility is that it stood opposite the front gates of that house, where there still remains a buttress-like stone construction, plainly very old though it is now topped by a modern water tank. An exactly similar structure stands isolated in the woods of Ashton Court beside Clarkencombe, and it is interesting that Philip Mede owned land there known as Combe Acre. There may be an architectural connection between the two. Behind the buttress at Failand Hill the land rises to an artificially level piece of meadow which could have formed the foundation of a part of the dwelling.

As like as not the Medes bought the land upon which to build Medes Place from the Berkeleys. The two families were well acquainted. Philip Mede had given Lord William Berkeley invaluable help in raising a muster of men to fight out a private quarrel with the Talbot family with whom he was in dispute over the ownership of lands in Somerset and Gloucestershire. That the families should be linked in marriage however was quite another matter and when Maurice Berkeley announced his intention of marrying Isabel, the merchant's gentle widowed daughter, his brother was furious. Her base blood, he raged, was quite unsuitable to flow in the veins of the heirs to the Berkeley title; her children, when they came, must never inherit the great estates. William fell out irrevocably with his brother, and to pay him out for contracting such a misalliance he arranged Maurice's disinheritance. At the same time he ordered matters to suit himself. He always hankered after titles, procuring many for himself in his lifetime. So, in return for the title of Marquis, he alienated the lordship and Castle of Berkeley to the then king, Henry VI. The propinquity of noble and merchant families in our little hamlet had resulted in the bitterest of family quarrels.

The rest of Maurice's life, and that of his wife, was coloured by this sad feud. After Lord William's death Maurice settled at Medes Place since he could live neither in Berkeley Castle nor in the manor at Portbury. Isabel had brought the Failand house to her husband as part of her dowry, with a twenty one year lease. Here in Failand he began the long fight to get back his title and property. John Smyth in his *Lives of the Berkeleys* calls him "Maurice the Lawier". We are reminded a little of poor Miss Flite in *Bleak House*, she who was always expecting a judgement shortly as she haunted the law courts about Lincolns Inn. Maurice Berkeley wore out the rest of his life in legal battles, long lawsuits which met with only partial success. He regained some of his properties but the house at Portbury was not among them, though it came back to the family at a later date. Smyth describes him in his last years:

> "With a milk-white head in his irksome old age, with a buckerom bag stuffed with law cases, in early mornings and late evenings walking with his eldest son between the Lower Inns of Court and Westminster Hall, following his law suites in his own olde person; not for himself but his posterity to regaine part of those possessions which a base brother had profusely consumed".

William Berkeley had not been known as Waste-All for nothing. Not only had the Berkeley Lordship been traded away but the whole inheritance was squandered. Poor Maurice's white head and worried looks were probably as familiar in Failand as in the London courts of law.

Maurice died in 1506, and his wife nine years later. Theirs had been a long and happy marriage strengthened no doubt by the sharing of the pain and suffering which their union had brought with it. There were four children, three sons and a daughter. One son, Thomas, became Governor of Calais, which was still a possession of the English crown. Another son, Maurice, was also in Calais at the time of his mother's death. His servant, Thomas Try, was in charge of Isabel's affairs and was with her when she died, not at Failand but at one of her other properties near Coventry, Calloughten. Thomas sent his master a full account of her funeral, and although the contents of his report is not strictly Failand history Isabel belongs firmly in our hamlet, and so the vivid and engaging account of her last journey is included here. The sixteenth century was well begun when she died but the story of her funeral with its blend of extreme piety and practical good sense is firmly rooted in the Middle Ages. The spelling has been modernised.

'This bill delivered to his right worshipful and special good Master, Sir Maurice Berkeley, Knight:
Pleaseth your good mastership, the ordering of the internment of my lady your mother hereafter followeth.
1. First when I perceived she began to draw from this life, I caused certain priests to say diverse orisons, and also to show her the Passion of Christ and the merits of the same, where unto she gave me marvellous goodly words, for aft her anneling (anointing with oil?) she came to good and perfect remembrance.
2. . . . Item: She was watched with prayer continually from Monday until Wednesday.
3. . . . Item: Ringing daily with all the bells continually; that is to say at St. Michaels 33 peels, at Trinity 33, at St. Johns 33, at Babylake because it was so nigh her life 57 peels.
4. . . . Item: Upon Sunday when her horse litter was appeled (summoned) and wax all other things ready, she was set forward after this manner.
5. First 30 women of her livery in black gowns and kerchiefs upon their heads, of one ell (1.25 yards) every kerchief, which was not furvelled neither hemmed because they must be known lately cut out of new cloth, and every woman bearing a taper of wax.
6. . . . Item; after them followed 33 crafts with their lights to the number of CC torches.
7. . . . Item; about her herself was her own servants bearing torches of clean wax, to the number of 30, in black gowns.
8. . . . Item; The order of friars, white and gray, with their crosses, next after the lights of the crafts.
9. . . . Item; Priests to the number of one C and more which went with their crosses next to the hearse.
10. . . . Item; after the horse litter V gentlewomen mourners.
11. . . . Item; after them Mr. Recorder, and I and Mr. Bonde and my cousin Porter, instead of the executors and surveyors.
12. . . . Item; then Mr. Mayor, the Mayor of Yeld, Aldermen, Sheriffs, Chamberlain and Wardens.
13. And so she was conveyed to the mother church, the priory, where she rested in the choir before the high altar all that night, and had there a solemn Dirge, and after the Dirge the Mayor and his brethren went into St. Mary's Hall, where a drinking was made for them: first cakes, comfits and ale, the second

course marmalet, snoker, red wine and claret, the third course wafers and blanchpowder with romney and mulkadele: and I thank God no plate nor spoons were lost, yet there were 22 dozen spoons.

14. Then upon Monday she set forward after Mass with the said lights and crafts, the said mourners riding in fed saddles and their horses draped with black, Mr. Recorder and I, Mr. Bond and Porter riding after them, and then Mr. Mayor, Aldermen, Sheriffs, Wardens and Chamberlains riding in like order as they were: And at Bynley Bridge met my Lord Abbot of Combe with his mitre sensing (incensing) the hearse, and in his company Mr. Brown, Mr. Broughton, and many other, ye may be sure to the number of V or VI thousand people, I am of a surety there was at every sitting above 11 or 12 messes (courses?) and the boards were divers times set, and Thomas Berkeley's priest saw the ordering of all.

                Your servant,
                Thomas Try.
Written at Calloughten the 16 day of April.

And so Isabel, born Mede, of Failand was laid to rest.

The de Faylands

There was an ancient family, the de Faylands, which took its name from the hamlet, and in the twelfth century Nicholas de Fayland became involved with the Berkeleys of Berkeley Castle and the mansion on Windmill Hill. The story was this. In 1189 Robert Berkeley took part in a conspiracy against the King, Henry II. As a result Henry seized Berkeley Castle and put in his own man, Hugo de Vivon, Lord of Bitton, as Constable. The King, always a lover of the law and a man to stand firm against aggressive behaviour in his subjects, seems to have recognized that Robert Berkeley was something of a bully, who threatened his Gloucestershire neighbours in a way the King did not like. Once his Constable was installed in Berkeley Castle he was told by Henry "to maintayne Nicholas de Fayland in the right of Margaret, the daughter of Otho, in the possession of her lands in Woodmancote and Dursley in as ample a manner as she had them before Lord Robert did disseize her, not permitting any wrong to be done to him or her, and to protect and defend them and theirs"[1]. In other words, it was Nicholas de Fayland's job to see that no further misconduct by Robert Berkeley should take place either towards Margaret or her father.

The family name, variously spelt, continues to appear in local records throughout the Middle Ages. In 1327 Augustine de Foyland was "assessed to the Exchequer lay subsidies at ii shillings". In the early fifteenth century Robert de Foiland's name appears in the Bristol City Archives as witness to some deeds, and a little later in the same century Thomas Foyland appears in the same capacity. The de Faylands, it seems, continued to be a considerable family throughout the Middle Ages.

Where did they live? It is not unreasonable to suppose that they would have lived in the Manor House of the hamlet from which they took their name. High up on the tableland of Upper Failand stands Manor Farm, a house probably built in Tudor times, with a beautiful circular staircase, and a stout oaken front door. Until twenty or thirty years ago it possessed other much older features which suggest a previous building on the site and the Rev. Masters in his *History of Wraxall* thinks the house "may possibly represent the ancient residence of the de Faylands". By the nineteenth century when Masters' history was written he tells us that the once proud

---

[1] Smyth's *Lives of the Berkeleys*.

house was "now degraded to a poor farmhouse but retaining in the arrangement of its rooms some manorial features, being entered from the South through a central passage, with the hall or living room on the West, and the kitchen on the East, the former built over a large cellar, while a circular staircase leads to the rooms above. Two small cherub's heads in low relief ornament a doorway outside . . . Lines of elevation in the soil point to former terraces and walls, and the existence of a somewhat large garden".

This lovely house remained a farm well into the present century though it has now become a private house. The cherub's heads mentioned by Masters have alas! disappeared along with an ancient stone-built chapel both of which must surely have belonged to the original mediaeval Manor. Their removal or destruction is sad indeed; all we have is a splendid photograph to prove their existence. At least, however we have a house still standing even if we know nothing of its history. It is the only dwelling left of those which once made up the 'considerable village' of Failand and so it finds a place in the next chapter.

'A considerable village'

The deepest mystery about the hamlet, the 'lost village', was the one which exercised the mind of Failand's only local historian, Mrs. Lucy Bowden until, in her last years, it became almost an obsession. She could not leave it alone. Her notes and papers show how as she grew older the possible explanations raced round and round inside her head, and the puzzle never resolved itself to her satisfaction. This chapter is a tribute to her tenacity; it is of necessity a pedestrian piece of work since the only way is to try, with hardly a fact to go on, to set out a step at a time what may have been the case. The hare is started by the Rev. Masters in his *History of Wraxall*. "There was once in Failand", he says, "a village, a considerable one . . . the residence of several families of importance, amongst whom were the Medes of Medes Place, and those of Madox, Baber, Harbord and Shepherd. All traces of their habitations have been destroyed and their sites forgotten".

Not quite. We have already seen one trace of the Mede mansion, the old buttress in the sloping field by Failand Hill House, the meadow immediately behind it absolutely smooth and level and perhaps the site of the main building. Rev. Masters mentions another piece of masonry which he saw in the nineteenth century, a gatepost with the name Madox Court carved upon it. This post was, he says, demolished in 1878. The 1830 Ordnance Map still marks Mad(d)ox Court and also a Maddox Farm, which must have been a part of the family estate. The house is shown near the present Lower Failand Farm, the farm is just over the border in Portbury.

With the Maddox family however, the Harbords and the Shepherds, we are dealing only with shadows, although Rev. Masters' book contains minute details of branches of the Harbord family outside Failand. With the Medes and the Babers we have some solid facts to rest on.

The Medes' position in our hamlet has already been established in the late Middle Ages. In the early sixteenth century, after the death of Isabel Berkeley in 1515, Medes Place was sold to a vigorous Welsh family called Morgan. Eve Wigan in her *Tale of Gordano* has plenty to say about them. They were, she tells us, Lords of the Manor of Easton-in-Gordano, where they had been since the days of Henry VI. It was Richard Morgan who bought the Manor of Easton in 1544, and "his sons and kinsmen spread themselves round in plenty; there are fourteen Morgans in the Baptism Register of Elizabeth's reign . . . There was a 'Thomas Morgan of Feilands in Wraxall, gent', who made a will leaving his 'house in Feilands, called

Medes Court, to his eldest son Edmund of Morgan.'" The change of name from Medes Place to the more impressive Medes Court is interesting. Such changes are still made in Failand when large properties change hands.

Of the Babers too we do know something. There is a will in Bristol City Archives, dated 1590, of a Catherine Baber 'of Faylon'. She appears to have been a wealthy woman and the wife of one William Baber. He outlived her, and his death is recorded in the Wraxall Church Register in the year 1606. Three children of a John Baber were baptised, William in 1566, Matthew in 1570 and Jane in 1575. John, the father, died ten years later. If we move a little way into the next century we have the death recorded in 1606 of Mrs. Elizabeth Baber 'of Faylon', the first time the name of the hamlet appears in the Wraxall Register. (The absence of detail in the register is characteristic, and its omission or inclusion though confusing seems to have little significance). The family appears once more in the Parish records with the registration of the three children of Robert Baber, Richard (1620), Robert (1629) and Bridget (1632).

About Robert, the father, we do know something. His name appears in a document quoted by Eve Wigan, which contains an account of the visitation of representatives of the College of Heralds to North Somerset in 1623. Under the claims entered in Portbury Hundred is one by 'Robert Baber gent. of Fayland', and Miss Wigan explains what was behind his claim to the title of gentleman, and that of the others whose names appear with him in the list of claimants. "Times were changing fast and new men sat in the seats of the mighty. The professional masters of ceremonies did their best to see that the new men were equipped with the ancient trappings. The rank of gentleman if not inherited had to be conferred by the sovereign, generally acting through the Royal College of Heralds . . . The College of Heralds sent out visitations throughout England at intervals until 1704 to ensure proper use of all titles and coats of arms, and three such came through Somerset in the sixteenth century". The first visitation in the next century seems to have been the one in 1623 which considered the claim of Robert Baber to the rank of gentleman. We are dealing here with a family which while it had wealth — Catherine Baber is described as having inherited a deal of money — needed to acquire gentility. As old families like the de Faylands declined into obscurity their place was taken by men of a different stamp. Masters tells us that the Babers' place of residence "was styled Saint Babers", and this splendidly pretentious name is most satisfactorily in keeping with the dignity which the family sought to demonstrate. Unlike Madox Court and Medes Court, the site of Saint Babers is not known to us, though it may have been at the top of Oxhouse Lane, opposite the two solitary cottages now standing on the right hand side of the lane. Local tradition says that these cottages were built with stone from a nearby mansion. Mrs. Bowden thought this mansion may have stood on the top of the somewhat artificial looking slope above the sheep dip. She cited as evidence the one tree growing there which she said gave the impression at a certain time every year that it had not enough moisture to sustain it properly, its roots resting in stony ground. If this was where the Baber house stood it was not far from the old home of the de Faylands.

The Manor must have remained a house of some importance; it retains today some sixteenth century features and no doubt the mediaeval building was altered and added to over the years. So a family of quality there would have formed part of the important community we are trying to establish. Mrs. Bowden, who walked her hamlet untiringly, and with her eyes well open, was very struck by the network of well marked footpaths in this area, linking one place of habitation with another. With the benefit of the first edition of the Ordnance Survey map, not available to her, we see these paths were considerable trackways in 1830, one of which joins the old Manor (marked but not named on the map) to the probable site of Saint Babers. These green lanes seem to suggest the ghostly framework of the lost village.

One more family, the Jubbes, have left their name behind as a marker to help our reconstruction. Jubbes Court, the present building, is an eighteenth century house standing at the head of the valley below Failand School. It has been variously known over the years as Court Farm, Jubbes Court, and Jubbes Court Farm, and the high scarp on the line of the old Wansdyke is still called Jubbes Wood. Rev. Masters is quite firm in calling the house "the old residence of the Jubbes". The Jubbes, like the Medes, were an important family in the Middle Ages and beyond. Matthew Jubbe was Sheriff of Bristol in 1495, Thomas was concerned with collecting taxes in the city in 1523, "a learned lawyer-man and of the Council of the Duke of Buckingham of Thornbury Castle"[1]. The likelihood is that the Jubbes, in the same way as the Medes, bought land from the Berkeleys on which to build their house. The convenience of a country residence so near Bristol would have had the same appeal for them as for the Medes, or any other rich merchant with business in the City. Traces of the original dwelling are hard to find. In the nineteenth century, Masters saw "some slight remains of foundations to the North . . . possibly those of a pond or garden". These are still visible and seem to suggest a series of ponds running into each other. There is abundant water from a lively little stream which still flows through the property. How long the Jubbes lived in Failand we do not know, but the house was probably rebuilt in the eighteenth century. It has a window of that period high in the end wall, facing the lane that runs past it

---

[1] quoted by Masters.

1 Exterior of the mediaeval chapel at Failand Manor, now disappeared. The carved cherubs' heads can be seen on the gateposts.

2 Ruined wall of the Berkeley oxhouse in Oxhouse Lane.

3 The original Failand Inn painted by Samuel Hieronymus Grimm in 1788

4 *Top:* The last relic of the 'considerable village', probably a part of Mede's Place.

5 *Bottom:* Aerial view of Failand House.

6 Lady Fry in her old age with Miss Agnes Fry standing beside her.

to Portbury. No doubt stone from the mediaeval building was incorporated, as it often is, in the later one. The immediate setting of the present house, tucked into the upper end of a lovely gentle valley is unchanged from the Middle Ages except for the school just above it and the Victorian stone cottage in the fields below.

The likely presence of a church serving these important houses in Failand is sometimes suggested, since seventeenth century maps show one marked in the vicinity. Yet there is no record of a living in Failand; Wraxall is the church which occasionally records the deaths of residents of 'Faylon' and John Smyth, in the sixteenth century, speaks of Failand, "in the Parish of Wraxall". It is of course possible that the little private chapel almost certainly attached to the Manor might have warranted a mention on the map.

By using the Wraxall Church register we can people the village with a few families other than the gentry; the references to Failand begin there in earnest in the seventeenth century. Ann Payne of Failand married Richard Hogge of the Citie of Bristow, dying in 1644, daughter of Edward Payne of Failand; Ann Mayes of Failand, wife of John, died in the same year. They had a servant with the charming name of Callanty. Her death is recorded in 1660 so perhaps she took care of John after his wife's death. In 1647 John Gaynor died, a miller of Failand; there was a mill somewhere in the neighbourhood. Some of these people may have died of the plague for in 1610 the whole Cox family, six of them, died of it in Wraxall, and among the books listed in the church inventory for 1634 is one called "A thanksgiving for staying of ye plague". Mrs. Bowden speaks of a plague burial ground in the fields at the top of Oxhouse Lane in Upper Failand. "A very old inhabitant told me that when his father brought him there as a small boy the field behind the shed (a workman's shed still there in Mrs. Bowden's time) had once been a burial ground." She tells us also that a lime kiln was once situated in the fields opposite the Sixty Acre development on the main Clevedon Road, lime being essential to destroy infected corpses. She kept a photograph of the ruined kiln.

One more little detail helps to breath some life into our picture of the village. It concerns a Welsh farmer, Fluellin, who though he lived just outside Failand must have been well known to everyone in the immediate vicinity. Well known because of the extraordinary difficulty the Somerset people found in getting their tongues (and their pens) round his name. We hear of Fluellin in John Smyth's account of the wastrel Thomas Berkeley, born in 1575, he who "far outran his income" and who without his father's consent, sold the remainders in the "three parkes of Portbury Manor with Fluellin's farm adjoining". This liquid Welsh name caused the clerks who made up the Wraxall Church Register infinite trouble. It appears there from 1576 onwards in no fewer than nine different spellings:

Fewelling, Flewellyn, Lluellinn, Fluellen, Llewellyn, Lewelling, Lleuellin, Fewelin and Lawellin.

No trace now remains of Saint Babers or the homes of the Harbords and the Shepherds. There was no trace of them by the beginning of the nineteenth century for not even a name on the ordnance map of 1830 suggests their presence. Only Maddox Court warrants a mention there and by 1878 the last of that was gone. All we have left is a house standing on the sight of Jubbes Court and the solitary buttress from Medes Court in the field on Failand Hill. The references to the Baber family in the parish register cease abruptly in the 1630s.

Why did all these great houses disappear so completely? The Civil War, fought over the whole of England from 1642 until 1649, must hold the answer. With a Royalist garrison on Battery Point defending Portishead fort and Bristol held first by the Roundheads, then the Royalists, and finally taken for Oliver Cromwell by General Fairfax, the countryside in this part of North Somerset must have been overrun by the soldiery, with Failand in the thick of it. When the Royalists were in the ascendant the Somerset Hundreds were required to raise £500 per week, an enormous sum in those days, and Portbury Hundred, which included Failand, had to find £121-10-6 of this per month. "Wretched Portbury Hundred, perpetually in default, would be liable to endless punitive forays from His Highness' (Prince Rupert) troop of horse. In nearly every village a defensive force of 'clubmen' was formed to fob off as best they could such foray."[2] As well as the damage and perpetual anxieties inflicted on the inhabitants of the village by Rupert's men, the big houses may have suffered attacks by either side during the course of the war, according to which party they supported. The great Berkeley mansion itself, up on Windmill Hill, was probably under siege at this time. It had passed by marriage to the Coke family of Norfolk in 1613 and the new owners had no interest in their distant possession. The total neglect of the house dates from this period and a few salvos from an enemy intent upon entering its gates may have accelerated the process.

No-one knew at the end of the Civil War in 1649 what lay ahead under the Protectorate of Oliver Cromwell. The owners of important properties in Failand, contemplating the damage to their homes and reflecting on the absence of a noble family on Windmill Hill to act as a shield against further lawlessness, probably decided to cut their losses and settle elsewhere. From this time must date Failand's reversion to a place of lesser importance, an inconsiderable hamlet; but Fate still had some surprises in store.

---

[2] Eve Wigan. *Tale of Gordano.*

Failand and the Picturesque

Anyone riding in a car or a bus along the main road which runs through upper Failand towards Clevedon finds his gaze impelled away from the course of the present road and away up to the right, where stands a large square house at the end of a driveway. It is the line of the original road which draws the eye; beside this road on the site of the 19th century house stood the old Failand Inn. This inn was certainly there, high up on Leigh Down, as early as 1687 and perhaps even earlier. It was owned then by Sir Halswell Tynte whose ancestors had lived for some generations in Wraxall, and who was related by marriage to the Babers. There was probably a Justice Room attached to the inn as early as 1672. Inns were commonly used by Justices of the Peace as places in which to hold Petty Sessions, and there is an order by two justices in the Quarter Sessions records of Charles II's reign dated at Failand in that year, 1672.

A hundred years later in 1788 this old inn turns up together with another local subject, the 'Fayland's Cross', in a collection of Somerset views painted by a considerable topographical and landscape artist Samuel Hieronymus Grimm. This was the time when the Picturesque was all the rage in art; the romantic ruin, the mis-shapen tree, the rough road through wild places spoke to the popular imagination. Even "the border of the road itself shaped by the mere tread of passengers and animals . . ; even the tracks of wheels (for no circumstance is indifferent) contribute to the picturesque effect of the whole."[1] What better then for a suitable subject than an ancient inn standing in isolation on a remote stretch of downland, thatched and gabled, its approach no more than a muddy lane? What better companion piece than the battered remains of an even more ancient cross, hardly a cross at all since only the base yet remained, desolate in an empty waste of fields with a sublime view spread out in the distance behind it?

In the first of Grimm's pictures the inn is shown as a whitewashed building long and low and extended on both sides by stable blocks. In through the door of one of these an ostler is leading a horse, and above one of the windows the words 'Failand Inn' are painted on the wall. A beautifully roomy wooden settle with a very high back stands to the left of the main entrance, a good place to have your drink on a fine day, sheltered

---

[1] Sir Uvedale Price. *An Essay on the Picturesque* 1794.

from the wind which always blows on top Failand. At right angles to the front door of the inn runs a boundary wall, its top protected by a sloping roof of a kind not often seen in these parts. An open-sided farm building sheltering some kind of farm cart is at the corner of the wall, and running parallel with the wall and in its shelter is a small bowling green — two men are having a game there. Beside the green is a strange irregular stone, mounted on some kind of plinth. Perhaps this was one of the last remaining standing stones left behind from the Bronze Age. We know from local historians that great prehistoric boulders stood near this spot until sadly they were broken up to make the new road early in the 19th century. Away in the distance the artist suggests with his brush the higher tree-fringed line marking the crest of the down.

Grimm's other picture, the old 'Fayland's Cross', is by no means as interesting a subject to paint. Cromwell's men were said to have knocked it about severely and little of it remained. To liven things up a bit the artist has introduced a picnic into the scene. Spread out on the flat surface of the smaller, upper stone is a bottle, a jug and what looks like a good sized joint of meat, a loaf and a sausage. There are two picnickers formally dressed and hatted, one seated on the grass and one standing. They are talking to each other, and spread out before them is a magnificent view numbered on the canvas and labelled thus across the top: 1. English Coast 2. St. George's Channel 3. Welsh Coast 4. Flatholm 5. Steepholm 6. Worl(e) Hill 7. Minehead Point 8. Severn River 9. Nailsea Moor 10. decoy 11. Fayland's Cross.

Plainly by the 18th century this was a favourite viewpoint and picnic spot — to eat out of doors was itself a delightfully unconstrained and rustic thing to do, the pleasure made complete by the vista spread out before one to complete the day's enjoyment. The history of the old cross would have added to the romance of the occasion for it was originally a resting place along a very ancient trackway, leading in pre-historic times from Maes Knoll Camp on Clifton Down to Cadbury Camp near Tickenham. The track must have continued in use for many centuries, long enough for a cross to be built in Christian times, though by the time of the picture it had fallen into disuse.

About the inn we have some interesting factual detail. A longhand note by the Rector of Wraxall in 1884 tells us that in the eighteenth century "a well-attended Neighbour-Gentlemen's Group used to dine there regularly." No doubt they made use, on a summer's evening, of the bowling green which Grimm has put into his picture. There may also have been another and larger green some way up behind the inn, for there is a flat field there on one side of Horse Race Lane which has always been known as the Bowling Green. It could be that this second green dated from much earlier days when Medes Court and other great houses stood in this part of

Failand and their owners laid out greens for their own amusement. Only the name now remains, and this scrap of dialogue heard in the lane near the field some fifteen or twenty years ago:

"Where be thee going then, Bill?

I be'est go'in to cut Bowling Green."

We know the particulars of some of the petty crime tried in the Justice Room of the inn in the early part of the nineteenth century. The sentences passed had the severity characteristic of that time. A child of ten, son of a poor widow, stole a few sprigs of lilac from a clergyman's garden and had two months on the treadmill. (Oliver Twist at about the same date was sentenced to receive three month's hard labour for stealing a pocket handkerchief.) Another punishment, though no doubt severe, had its funny side. George Alvis (a local name still) was "committed to the house of correction for one month for wilfully throwing a snake at a timid young lady on whom he had played similar tricks such as pitching toads and mice at her." One's sympathy is all with the young lady. A third case was straightforward theft. Two women were committed to Ilchester Gaol for stealing several hundred yards of bleach linen at Ashton, and the two women receivers were given a similar sentence.

Quite a different matter of particular local interest was also heard at the inn in the early nineteenth century; a special court was summoned to Failand to determine the value of the four and a quarter acres required to make the approach to the proposed Clifton Suspension Bridge, presumably so that proper compensation could be paid to the owner of the land.

A regular annual event was the licensing season held by the magistrates at the inn from 1788 onwards. Private individuals owned public houses in those days — the first owner we hear of at Failand is Sir Halswell Tynte in the seventeenth century; in the early nineteenth century the inn was rebuilt as we shall see by George Penrose Seymour Esquire of Belmont.

We know very little of the actual people who came to the inn or who lived there but there are a few names. The innkeeper in 1710 was Will Watts; he had a daughter Eleanor who died in 1710, her death recorded in the Wraxall Church register. In 1823 the landlord's name was Pearce. A daughter Mary Ann was born to Joseph, "Failand's innkeeper", and his wife Mary in that year, and four years later, in 1827, they had a son Joseph. They almost certainly had relatives farming nearby, for Benjamin and Margaret Pearce had a daughter Emma at Failand in 1830 and Benjamin was a farmer. Sailors must have frequented the place; someone seeking hands for a privateer in 1785 advised able-bodied men seeking a ship to apply to "the Fayland Inn, Leigh Down".

Of the farmers who certainly drank and dined there one must surely have been the tenant or owner of Failand Farm. This beautiful dignified early 18th century house was built in 1714 by John and Elizabeth Clapp who carved their names over its front door. Tucked away in a smiling wooded valley below the exposed ridge of Leigh Down it still stands with its graceful circular staircase and original high silled windows, one of the few really old houses left in the hamlet. On the Ordnance map of 1830 it is the only farm named in Failand; a cluster of buildings shown beside it suggest the presence of Ferney (or Funny) Row, a line of cottages still inhabited today, one of which is certainly contemporary with the farm itself.

Although the inn must have been a wonderfully lively place: gentlemen meeting for a convivial evening with bowls outside in summer and snug by the fire in winter, sailors looking for a new berth, criminals arriving to stand trial, magistrates, the people of the hamlet and passing travellers. And where is it now if it stood in its heyday where now stands Failand Lodge farm, foursquare to the present main road, a solid respectable early Victorian dwelling? The answer is to be found round the back in the farmyard. A photograph of the outbuildings there taken by Mrs. Bowden in the 1950's suggests very closely the old frontage of the inn as we see it in Grimm's watercolour drawing and the pointed arch of the front door in the picture is echoed in the arch-like outline of the windows and door of the farm building. Inside this block of buildings the remains of the prisoner's dock can still be seen standing in a long solidly built room which must have housed the court, the Justice Room. We know that some rebuilding took place about 1801. It was undertaken by a George Penrose Seymour Esquire, of Belmont, probably the owner at that time. This rebuilding must be that part of the present farm which forms its back premises, facing as they do onto a courtyard in the manner of an inn. The front of the house is puzzlingly different in style, solid dignified early Victorian facing foursquare towards the present main road, as we have seen, an apparent addition to Seymour's new building. The explanation of this mixture of styles lies in the final years of the inn's story. The downland which lay about it was enclosed in 1812 and the line of the road was altered so that the Failand Inn stood in a quiet backwater instead of poised as it used to be on the main thoroughfare to Bristol ready to welcome the traveller. In 1835 it closed and after a brief period as a playhouse run by a Dr. Wallace — the courtroom would have served well as a small theatre — the place became a school, a reputable boy's boarding school which prospered for half a century and numbered amongst its pupils the famous cricketer, W.G. Grace. The imposing house which catches our eye now as we drive across upper Failand must surely have been added at the beginning of the new chapter in the life of this high corner of the hamlet. It would have supplied the necessary dignity needed and more practically the accommodation necessary to board more than a hundred boys. The story of this school comes next.

Endpiece. The new inn in Failand, the one we now have on the main road through to Clevedon, was built about 1860, its first licensees the Lott sisters. In the interval between the closing of the old inn in 1835 and the opening of the present one anyone wanting beer or cider would probably have obtained it from one or other of the farms in the neighbourhood. In 1830 the Beerhouse Act had been passed which enabled "any householder assessed to the poor rate to obtain from Excise on payment of two guineas a year a licence authorising him to sell beer by retail in his dwelling house, for consumption on or off the premises."[2]

---

[2] Paterson's 'Licensing Acts'.

Two schools

A farmer or a tradesman looking for a good education for his son in our part of North Somerset in the early 19th century would have been in some difficulty. He would probably be hoping for something better than the kind of primary teaching provided in some rural areas by the church schools. These were built and maintained by the Anglican church and, until state primary education was augmented in 1870 by the Board schools, paid for out of the rates, the voluntary church schools were the only kind generally available to the poor. There was a schoolroom of some kind in Failand as early as 1839; the main school building was put up by Wraxall Church in 1847. It must have served the children of farm labourers, estate workers and others at similarly poorly paid level in society.

Those with more money and with ambition for their sons may have considered what Bristol had to offer; the answer at that time was not very much. The endowed schools, with which the city was well provided, Colston's, Queen Elizabeth's and the like, catered only for local pupils, so the sons of farmers and well-to-do tradespeople outside the city would not easily have found a place there. Grammar schools were traditionally for the very bright boys of every walk of life but even supposing a country lad were to be accepted, Bristol Grammar School in the early 19th century was at a very low ebb. There were one or two good private schools in Bristol, including one kept by a non-conformist minister, and some other good schools of the same kind in the country. Now, as the result of the enterprise of a "committee of neighbouring farmers and gentlemen", Failand had such a school of its own. This committee, perhaps an offshoot of the gentlemen's dining club which used to meet regularly at the Failand Inn during the previous century, put up the then considerable sum of £600 to found a school for the sons of farmers and tradespeople. As we already know they leased the premises of the old Failand Inn for their undertaking, and probably soon added the large square house to the old building to give workable accommodation for their purpose. They called the establishment Failand Lodge School. It is this considerable property, now a farmhouse still called Failand Lodge, which we see from the main road today.

We have only to look at Failand Lodge as it stands now, on the crest of high downland in the clear bracing air, to feel its possibilities as a boarding school. One could almost write the prospectus. Throughout its life of some forty years the school had but one headmaster, Jesse Talbot. There is not much doubt that, as is often the case with small but thriving schools, the success of the place was due to the personality of its head. I have heard an old inhabitant of our hamlet refer not to Failand Lodge but Talbot Lodge; she would certainly have heard it so called, probably by her mother or grandmother and this suggests that the school and its head were very closely associated in the minds of those who knew them. Jesse Talbot must have been a fairly young man when he came with his wife Marianne to build up the new enterprise. Three children were born to them quite soon after they arrived — Georgina appears in the year 1840, Horatio Beauchamp, no doubt named after Lord Nelson, comes next, and Emma (surely *not* after Lady Hamilton?) in 1843.

The committee of farmers and gentlemen were in overall charge of affairs, rather like a board of governors, but Mr. Talbot ran the school for them. The secretary of this committee for many years was Edward Protheroe Vaughan, youngest son of Rev. James Vaughan, the Rector of Wraxall in the first part of the 19th century. Mr. Vaughan was his father's curate and later, in 1857, himself became Rector. In some notes written in 1884 he tells us that he gave a lesson in religious knowledge at Failand Lodge School every Monday morning. The total number of boys educated at the school during its forty-one years was some twelve hundred. There would have been between a hundred and a hundred and twenty boys there at any one time. We know too that only boarders were taken. The Rev. Masters in his history of Wraxall says that as a boarding school for boys of the middle class it was among the first of its kind to appear. The public schools in the early nineteenth century were of course still the preserve of the aristocracy and the upper classes.

The curriculum in both public and grammar schools at this time was narrowly classical; Latin and Greek were predominant. The governors of Failand Lodge included practical men, farmers and others, who would have been aware of a demand, in an England beginning to grow wealthy and powerful, for a broader and more up-to-date education. Dotheboy's Hall, in *Nicholas Nickleby*, is a caricature of a school, but it is in essence the same kind of small private establishment as Mr. Talbot's. Dickens gives us some of the curriculum: use of the globes (geography), Latin, English spelling and botany, all are offered by Mr. Wackford Squeers, the horrible headmaster, in his own inimitable fashion.

"B-o-t, bot, t-i-n, tin, bottin, n-e-y, ney, bottiney, noun substantive, a knowledge of plants. When the boy has learned that bottiney means a knowledge of plants he goes and knows 'em." (That is he weeds the garden. Squeers kept his boys busy). "That's our system, Nickleby."

Certainly not Jesse Talbot's way, but no doubt he covered the same range of subjects.

We know a little about some of the pupils at the school. The sons of the farmer at Charlton Farm were there, and we have a handwritten note by the grandson of one Hartley Thomas Batt of Backwell, telling us that his grandfather was among the first batch of pupils. He started at the school in 1841. Mr Batt's father was also a pupil and so too his son. The family plainly thought well of Failand Lodge. An old school friend of Mr Batt senior wrote frequent letters from New Zealand reminiscing about "old Jesse Talbot". Affection for the school and its traditions had begun to grow.

The "star of the old boys" as he was known was W.G. Grace. He makes an appearance on the printed programme of the Sports Day for 1869. He had left the school by then and was a young man of twenty-one. On that Monday afternoon in May — the 24th — he acted as Judge and Handicapper, and his name also appears as an entrant in the 220 yards Hurdle Race (ten flights) and the two mile visitors' race. It must have been the jolliest of occasions, and it is not hard to imagine the delighted reverence of the pupils (and probably their fathers too) for this god-like figure. The records tell us that by the year of this particular sports day W.G. had already as a cricketer done unbelievable deeds for such a young man: one hundred and seventy runs at Brighton against the Gentlemen of Sussex, and in another match a century in both innings. All honour to him for returning to his old school and not being too grand to take part in the sports events that early summer afternoon in Failand.

We have one memory of Talbot's school which links it to us in the twentieth century. A very old Failand inhabitant told me that her mother could recall on a Sunday seeing Mr. and Mrs. Talbot driving down to Wraxall Church in their small carriage closely followed by a long crocodile of boys. They were expected to walk down to Wraxall and what's more to walk 'in step'. By this time Jesse Talbot would have been an old man, probably over seventy. When the second lease on Failand Lodge ran out (it belonged to the Gibbs, Lord Wraxall's family) it was not renewed. Other schools by now probably met the needs of the neighbourhood. Clifton College received its charter in 1877 and Bristol Grammar School had come to better days. The old school became for a time a laundry for the Tyntesfield estate at Wraxall; the amount, complexity and high finish required for the linen in large Victorian households must have been considerable. Very soon however, in 1882, the house and grounds were leased to a market gardener, Mr. Down. His son eventually purchased the property from Lord Wraxall, and his grandson lives there to this day, the last real market gardener left in Failand.

Down in Lower Failand all this time the village children from poorer homes were getting their education. We have already heard of a schoolroom in the hamlet in 1839, at about the same time that Jesse Talbot's school was starting up. It is referred to in a licence issued by the Bishop of

Bath and Wells which makes it possible to use "a place within the hamlet called and known as the School Room . . . . for the Celebration of Divine Service." Many people plainly found the journey to Wraxall Church inconvenient. Whether this schoolroom was run as a fully fledged village school we do not know, or where it stood; perhaps it was in the small building which later became the teacher's house. It may only have been a place where a village woman taught a few children their letters, but more likely something more than that, since it was plainly considered suitable to use it for Divine Service. In the birth entries of the Parish Register under Failand about this time, in 1844, there is mention of a Moses Curtis, schoolmaster, whose wife had a son and later a daughter. It is possible that he could have taught the children of the hamlet, though he is just as likely to have been a master at Failand Lodge. However that may be, the school proper as we see it today was built in Lower Failand in 1847.

Failand School is beautifully placed at the head of the valley just above Jubbes Court. It is built of our local pinkish purple stone and stands charmingly surmounted by its little bell tower, a distinctive silhouette against the skyline when viewed from the fields below. Solidly attached to it but different in style is the diminutive schoolhouse, dwelling place for headmaster or mistress and probably a few years older than the school building itself. The Anglican church at Wraxall must have considered by 1847 that there was a need for a proper local school in Failand. Perhaps the small congregation who met to worship in the original schoolroom made the point personally to the Rector or Curate taking the service. At all events a site was purchased from the Blagrave family (who had owned land locally for more than a century), the school was built, and for the next one hundred and thirty eight years the valley was filled with the echoing sound of children's voices and laughter, and the brisk ringing of the bell to mark the end of playtime. Then, after July 1985[1] it was heard no more and those who live in the fields below have felt the poorer for it. Those who wonder what it was like to go to a little school like Failand in the 19th century can do no better than read the village tales of the Victorian author Charlotte Yonge; she captures the experience at first hand. We have lively memories and to spare of the part played by the school in the life of the neighbourhood in the 20th century as we shall see later.

The school would have stood in its early years with only Jubbes Court Farm for company. An older farm stood where now New Farm looks down on the dip. The building of the great neo-Gothic church and chantry close by in the latter part of the 19th century probably gave the little hamlet as much of a centre as it had ever known; the addition in the 20th century of

---

[1] When the school was closed down.

the Failand Estate houses reinforced the illusion. But the main road which those who built St Bartholomew's church had expected to run by its porch did not materialise. Church, chantry and school remained in lovely isolation as they still do today.

The presence of two schools in one small hamlet is interesting but not extraordinary. However, there came to Failand in the late nineteenth century one remarkable piece of educational good luck. The Frys, a Quaker family all of whom were clever and cultured in their individual ways, came to live in Failand House, at first in 1875 as a holiday home and later as their permanent and only residence. The family stayed in Failand one way and another for sixty years. They loved learning for its own sake and were strongly imbued with the Quaker tradition of service to the community. As a result they opened the eyes and ears of the country people living in what was then an isolated and remote community to pursuits and interests which would otherwise have remained a closed book to them. The story of this remarkable family and its influence on the little hamlet where they lived for so long is given in the following chapter.

The Frys of Failand

The Fry family, parents and children, lived in Failand House for over sixty years. There is a yellowing newspaper cutting showing the last of them, Miss Agnes, standing outside the Home Farm in 1935 on the occasion of the Silver Jubilee of George V and Queen Mary. Miss Fry, having given an oak tree to mark this important event and having made sure it has been properly planted, has moved forward and is, in the words of the reporter, "addressing the assembly". One may imagine her earnestly drawing her audience's attention — the teachers, pupils, and parents of the village school — to the significance of the ceremony, in the strange deep tones of her well-remembered voice. She is a gaunt figure, clad in a long dark coat, flat black straw hat well pulled down, her hair scraped up out of sight beneath it, and sensible flat buttoned shoes. She is in her sixties; she first came to Failand when she was four. The Fry family made an indelible mark upon the life of the scattered hamlet from Victorian times till just before the Second World War. Their story is best begun with Agnes' father, Edward, who spent his boyhood in Bristol.

Most people associate the name Fry with the chocolate and cocoa business, and indeed Edward Fry was born in the house next to the original modest factory built in Union Street in 1795. The year of his birth was 1827 and he was the son of Joseph, himself involved in the family business. His early life in the city is interesting. As a little boy he remembered standing on the back stairs at home watching the flames rise from buildings set on fire by the Bristol Rioters. That was in 1831. When he was ten and on holiday in Weston-super-Mare he saw Brunel's steamship 'Great Western' leave on its maiden voyage across the Atlantic. On this same holiday he made an expedition with his family to Banwell, to see a collection of prehistoric bones belonging to a quaint old man named Beard, and he records that the visit "made a lively impression on my mind".

Here began Edward Fry's interest in science, an interest which concentrated in adolescence upon anatomy. He had a consuming passion for bones. A few years after the Banwell expedition there was a find of prehistoric relics in one of the limestone quarries on Durdham Down. Edward paid many visits to the site and talked earnestly and to some

---

[1] Writings of Sir Edward Fry.

purpose to the quarrymen there. For after the bulk of the discovery had gone to the Bristol Museum "there were some crumbs left, some of which fell into our hands . . . these I carefully studied."[1]

The fragments were arranged in two drawers of an anatomical cabinet, eventually finding their way also into the Museum. At nineteen, Edward wrote a paper on the skeleton of the Agile Gibbon, Hylobates Agilis, which he had studied at Clifton Zoo, and this was read before the Zoological Society in London. His most precious treasure, given to him and his brother by a Bristol doctor friend, was a human skeleton. The two young men carried the bones back to the family house in Charlotte Street in a hansom cab; it was carefully sited in the basement, suspended over a stand and surrounded by a moveable curtain.

Edward had left his school in Bristol at fifteen, and so that he might gain experience of the business world in which his family had their interests he was put to work in a firm of sugar brokers. Here he stayed until he was twenty, and during this time he read widely and deeply at home: classics, history, philosophy. A chance meeting at Charlotte Street with a Quaker lawyer, John Hodgkin, awoke his interest in the law as a profession, and he soon went to London to read for the Bar. He kept his scientific interests alive however, in a hundred different ways — the careful recordings of the rainfall charted by him into his extreme old age are still extant (Mr. Bert Roberts of Backwell has them) — yet he never regretted his choice of career, which remained for him "one of the noblest of human callings"[2]. The law was nonetheless his job, not his life. He always took proper holidays away from it, never worked on Sunday, and always when he could came home by six o'clock in the evening to his family. He was above all a family man.

In 1859, after a courtship lasting two years he married a beautiful girl, Mariabella Hodgkin. Like the Frys she was of Quaker stock, of the same distinguished family as the lawyer, John. Edward was devoted to her throughout their long lives. "I was only in love once", he told an old lady who had asked him how often he had lost his heart to a woman. "How dull of ye!" she replied. "That once lasted well over sixty years", was his answer[2]. The babies came along at fairly regular intervals. First came a son, Portsmouth, who bore a family name, shortened by his brothers and sisters to Porty. Then Mariabella, named after her mother, and like her very good looking, the only good looking one of all the girls, though all the Fry daughters in later life had a peculiar distinction of voice and bearing. Next came Joan; one may imagine the dreadful upset when as a small girl she lost an eye in a nursery accident, catching it upon the ear of the rocking horse.

---

[2] Sir Edward Fry's own account quoted in *Memoirs of Sir Edward Fry* by Agnes Fry.

Alice, who followed her, died when she was only four, but her parents grieved for her many years afterwards. Roger, the second son, was born next, then "the twinges" (Roger's word for them) Isabel and Agnes. Sara Margery and the baby Ruth, born when Lady Fry was over forty, completed the family. After her last child Lady Fry began that anxious care of her own health which she sustained into a long old age. She lived to be ninety seven.

All these children were born in London, in a house in Highgate, and here and later in Bayswater they grew up. It was their father's sensible custom, however, each year to rent a holiday house and here the lawyer's family would spend the many weeks of the long vacation. In 1874 the business of renting gave way to something more permanent. A place was heard of, perhaps through Fry relations, which sounded just what was wanted. It was called Failand House. Near Bristol, it was yet completely rural, approached only by deep, narrow lanes. It stood four hundred feet above the Bristol Channel, in a splendid situation. Sir Edward bought it and the two hundred acres which went with it, and in 1875 the family gathered there for their first holiday.

The house was in some ways unprepossessing. Built in the early eighteenth century as a gentleman's residence and owned for many years by Abraham Elton Esquire[3] of the well known family of Clevedon Court, it seems to have declined in dignity somewhat by the mid-nineteenth century, being referred to in one account as a farmhouse. The rectangular cellars which still run under the house suggest that originally it was that kind of neat, box-like building familiar to us in eighteenth century prints. By the time the Frys bought it, it had acquired many additions and outbuildings; the words "straggling" and "irregular" are used to describe it. It was built in the pinky-grey sandstone of the district. The front faced northwards making the rooms on that side rather gloomy but any shortcomings were almost entirely redeemed by the view. From its commanding height the house looked straight across the Bristol Channel. Agnes who looked out from the house across so many years knew every detail.

> "Behind the great stretch of water formed by the two rivers (Avon and Severn) and the Bristol Channel lie the ranges of the Welsh hills; the valleys of the Usk and the Wye, the lofty Brecon Beacon and the Forest of Dean, the cliffs of Aust, where St Augustine met the Welsh Christians, are all visible from the house or lawn, and the ever-changing lights and shadows on the waters, the great variation of the tides — a marked feature

---

[3] An old stone still standing in 'Fry's' woods is inscribed Hathway's Boundary 1775. The Hathway family may have been the previous owners. The name Hathway appears in Wraxall Parish registers.

of this district — the summer sunsets flaming behind the hills, their winter snows, the vividness of their details before the coming rain, the mists which reveal unsuspected hollows and folds — all these were no small pleasure to the owner of the house . . ."[4]

The back of the house, sunny and altogether less severe, overlooked the main gardens which were undistinguished when the Frys first came to Failand. Later, Sir Edward set his own mark upon them. The land which came with the property was extremely beautiful, acres of woods, copses, gentle hills and flowery fields, of a comeliness it would be hard to better anywhere in England, and all set amidst glorious distant views. There were scattered cottages and farms for which the new landlord was responsible. The Fry land was curiously intermingled with the estate of the Gibbs family of Wraxall and when Sir Edward bought Failand House he did his best to sort matters out with them, simplifying boundaries as best he could.[5]

To the Fry children gathered in Somerset for the first time in 1875 the house and grounds must have been a delight. The eldest of them, Portsmouth, was by now fourteen, the other son Roger was ten, and the girls ranged from young adolescence to babyhood. There were Fry and Hodgkin cousins galore to play with in and about Bristol — the family could muster sixty — and there was much coming and going. One cousin, Nellie Hodgkin, remembered Margery as "a little woman of the world . . . dashing through that formidable door, and reappearing with a piece of bread and cheese for each of us"[6]. The best place of all to play was Durbin's Batch, a small rounded hill rising up from the bluebell woodland threaded by a little stream. Here the children built a den and roofed it with bracken; here they made a water-wheel in the stream. Roger, years afterwards, named his Guildford house after this lovely familiar corner of his father's estate. It was Sir Edward's favourite.

There were plenty of splendid places within reasonable distance for picnics and expeditions. Margery aged twelve spent a very satisfactory day somewhere on the coast, probably near Weston. She gave an accurate account of it in a letter to her parents.

"Right out over the rocks and mud I found lots of sea-anemones, one was all over rosy red, some were grey and red, green and red-grey. I brought one dull little fellow on a loose stone up to

---

[4] *Memoirs of Sir Edward Fry* by Agnes Fry.
[5] This confusion can still be traced in existing deeds of Failand properties.
[6] quoted by Enid Huw Jones in her book *Margery Fry*.

7 Failand House (drawn by Elisabeth Robinson).

8 The old bell tower once used to summon the estate workers at Failand Hill House.

9 An early picture postcard of Failand Church, stamped 1909.

10 At the centre of Lower Failand, Failand School and Schoolhouse with the church behind.

11 George and Sarah Emery at the gate of Stone Cottage with two members of their family.

Ruth (the baby) and left him in a pool by her, where he opened out so that she could watch him, as Harry (the nurse) did not like her to go out on the rocks, as they were slippery"[7].

Sometimes their father took the children further afield. Once, he, Isabel, Agnes, and a nursery maid, caught a steamer at Avonmouth and went down the Bristol Channel to Lynmouth. Isabel later wrote an account of the adventure. The sea trip was rough and she and Agnes were

> "the worse for the tossing, but when we found ourselves in the little inn with the sound of the charming River Lyn in our ears all night, and were introduced to our father's delight in the joys of bilberry pie and Devonshire cream, we began to share his enthusiasm"[8].

No wonder Isabel and Agnes both loved their father. On another occasion they travelled with him by hired carriage across Devon staying each night in a small inn and ending up in Princetown, near the great prison. This was naturally interesting to Sir Edward, but the two girls spent an anxious night, fearful that escaped prisoners might be lurking behind the stuffy old garments crowded into their bedroom cupboard.

More formally, and as the children grew older, there were croquet and tennis parties, again with the cousins. Occasionally the Fry children must have hankered for companions outside the family circle. Nonetheless there was one household of Frys of whom Isabel at least thoroughly approved. These were the Frys at Goldney House in Clifton, and Isabel, always the difficult one at home, relished the indulgent atmopshere she found over the Bridge, the escape from supervision and from the rigid pattern of life at Failand.

> "Their scheme of life was in every way more ample than ours, their nurseries better equipped . . . The garden was a paradise, with a grotto, a big pond, high swings, dangerous walks on the top of vast lean-to greenhouses, with a holly hedge on the only protected side (a test of secret courage). There were ponies in the stables and cows in the fields and everywhere reigned a sense of freedom. One could play whip tops in the beautifully paved hall, one could finger the Grinling Gibbons' carving over the dining room mantelpieces, and one could eat as much as one liked in the kitchen garden"[6]

Yet there was a great deal of fun to be found at home if you were prepared

---

[7] A letter quoted by Enid Huw Jones: op. cit.
[8] Quoted in *Isabel Fry*, by Beatrice Curtis Brown.

to observe the rules. Permission must be asked for out of the ordinary ploys, and if parents were back in London then one must write and ask for it. Margery, so often the leader among the other children, wrote to her mother in London: "Ruth and I want to have a seed-sale. May we have some of the common seeds from the garden?" Permission granted, the affair went ahead. A preliminary announcement read as follows:

> "Messrs Francisteurs: the profits of the sale will be given to the Children's Bible Society, except that realised by S.M. Fry, who will sell some Honesty Seeds, the products of her garden"[9]

Indoor amusements were many. Bible clocks and texts were painted, there was dressing up (but no acting, an activity frowned upon by Quakers), flute and embroidery lessons. Every now and then, not too often, Lady Fry bought out the old Chinese lacquer cabinet which she had had since she was three. There were nine drawers, one for each child; poor little dead Alice's drawer contained only one small alphabet letter. The others filled up over the years with mementoes chosen and kept by the mother for each of her children, and each child was given a chance to inspect his or her own special drawer. The particular spicy smell lingered in the memories of all the Frys. Once Margery was allowed to tame a jackdaw, and Jack Daw went back to London where he flew down from his owner's shoulders at parties and pecked the ankles of strange children.

All in all, the young Frys seem to have enjoyed a satisfying childhood at Failand. There were, it is true, none of the unsupervised larks which Isabel described with such relish at Goldney House, but many children prefer a certain amount of discipline and routine since it demonstrates to them that grown ups really care about their welfare. Lady Fry was particularly good with babies and young children. Shy and reserved in society, she only entertained "duty" guests outside her own family circle — her garden parties are remembered as stiff. Yet in the nursery and the schoolroom she was at home, interested and interesting, teaching her young ones to observe with accuracy (as Margery did the sea anemones) the natural beauties of their country surroundings, explaining the stars, encouraging the music, the embroidery, the painting. Of course she insisted, since this was a Victorian household, that the children present themselves punctually at meals, scrubbed, controlled, not "rompy". On Sundays at exactly ten o'clock the family drove down Failand Lane towards Portbury on their way to Meeting at Portishead. The "whorlicoat", an oval six-seated vehicle always used for this journey, was so punctual that the local people

---

[9] Quoted in *Margery Fry* by Enid Huw Jones.

could, and did, set their clocks by it. Yet Margery, looking back from middle age, remembered even Sunday with favour, "solemn yet richly textured."[10]

When we next focus upon the family it is 1892. Seventeen years have passed and Sir Edward is about to retire from the Bench, promptly at sixty-five, as he always said he would. Much has changed. Failand House remained the holiday home during all this time but the mainstream of life was of course in London. A sad blow had fallen upon the Frys. The eldest boy, Portsmouth, full of promise at school, and the apple of his father's eye, had contracted in late adolescence an illness, from which he grew steadily worse, deteriorating both mentally and physically, finally becoming confined to a wheelchair, cared for by a permanent valet-attendant. The poor father's disappointed hopes shifted to his second son, Roger. This boy, at school at Clifton College, showed there an aptitude for science which won him a rare scholarship to Cambridge. There, to Sir Edward's horror, the young man promptly forsook science for art (quite justifiably as it turned out since he became not only a good artist but the outstanding art critic of his time). His father, who was known to prefer the merits of a coloured photograph to those of a painting, could not understand or accept what his son had done. Nonetheless, good father that he was, he made Roger an allowance which enabled him to do what he most wanted, to travel in Europe and study great pictures.

Among the girls, Mariabella inherited her mother's love of babies and young children. She was allowed to take a nurse's training, practising her skills upon members of the family. Her disposition was gentle and biddable, and as we have seen she was the only daughter to inherit her mother's looks. A photograph of her as a young woman shows her much as her mother must have looked at the same age, her carriage upright and graceful, her figure shapely, yet sturdy and beautifully proportioned. At about the time of her father's retirement, when she was in her early thirties, Mariabella had a suitor. He was a young doctor whom she had met ar Weston, probably when she stayed there to help nurse Portsmouth. The young man came to Failand to see Sir Edward, but he was sent away, and did not come again. Young men generally were not encouraged by the Fry parents. Joan, the next girl, was by the eighteen nineties an ardent Quaker, the only religious enthusiast in the family. She was also an accomplished horsewoman, riding in the Row while in London, and at Failand a familiar sight sidesaddle in an immaculate grey habit, always riding a grey horse. Of the twins, Agnes grew up under the handicap of severe deafness and some malformation of the palate. She was probably the cleverest of all the

---

[10] Quoted by Enid Huw Jones: op. cit.

children, but she found her contentment in joining in her father's intellectual pursuits. She was devoted to him. Isabel was awkward and somewhat plain and of all Lady Fry's daughters the one most at odds with her.

To Isabel her mother seemed "a swamping and captivating individual — both impatient with unfemininity yet seeming not to encourage her daughters to make the best of themselves"[11] Fortunately for Isabel she made her escape from this, for her, too oppressive influence, just before her father's retirement. She went to teach at Roedean, founded a few years previously, and never came home to live again, eventually starting a progressive, unorthodox school of her own. Margery, always a sunny attractive personality, was the leader among her brothers and sisters, and closest to her mother. She had been allowed to go away to school for a short period, also to Roedean, where she delighted in the companionship and the excellent teaching. For her it was a time of "complete bliss". She had returned just before her father's retirement. Ruth, the youngest child, still only in her teens, seems, like Mariabella, Joan and Agnes to have been content at home.

So in 1892 Sir Edward retired with promptitude from the Bench and turned eagerly away from London to live permanently on his Somerset property. This had been his intention from the beginning. For all his deep loving concern for his family he had always been a man with a multitude of interests and a rich, full interior life of his own. He was perfectly equipped to enjoy to the full his "declining years". Only Isabel and Roger of all the now grown up family of children did not come to Failand. Isabel had left for Roedean and Roger, after leaving Cambridge, found it impossible to live at home. The atmosphere there seemed to him, already moving in Bohemian circles in London, unbearably oppressive.

The rest of the family, together with all the paraphernalia of a great household, came down from London to settle at Failand House. Since a judge, even though retired, might be expected to write and receive important letters, a post office was opened in one of a pair of cottages[12] opposite the Home Farm, to deal with them. (This little office also kept a few jars of boiled sweets under the stairs to sell to customers. Apart from a makeshift grocery shop run from a farm this was the only shop in the hamlet). Sir Edward turned his attention first to the house, and to the construction of a large library. Agnes, in her memoir of her father[13] tells us it was "a handsome room capable of housing some four thousand volumes, and in this pleasant sunny room which was a great joy to him,

---

[11] '*Isabel Fry*' by B. Curtis Browne.
[12] Known until a few years ago as "The Old Post Office".
[13] *Sir Edward Fry* opus cit.

many hours of his last years were spent, studying alone, or with one of his daughters; and to this sanctum any ailing member of his family often received a special invitation. This room indeed was an environment of his own creation, as much an expression of his own nature as the nest of the bird . . . the different classes of books were presided over by busts of representative authors placed in recesses designed for them"[14]

Roger came down down to give his advice and assistance. His father had added a verandah or loggia to the back of the house, and at one end of this Roger painted a fresco with the figures of Plato and Socrates, now, since the conversion of the house into units, unfortunately over-painted. He also designed the interior woodwork. As to the garden, Sir Edward "made considerable additions including a small pinetum . . . the great feature of his garden was of his own designing — a straight walk, tiled with red bricks and with wide borders of grass and herbaceous plants leading to a small pond behind which Diana stands robing herself". (The statue is still in the grounds of Failand House. At one time when the house was being developed into a riding centre it was nearly destroyed but was rescued by Mr. Bert Roberts, who carried it bodily to a place of safety). "This walk was my father's quarterdeck; here he would pace up and down and talk, or do a constitutional mile, twenty two times the length of the path on uncongenial winter days . . . He took an almost personal interest in his trees, whether those he found there — the great Portuguese laurel on the lawn, and the group of Scotch Firs in a field which formed a landmark to vessels in the Channel — or those he planted; and when one Sunday morning a great Western gale made havoc among them, his face as he watched the fall of a cherished cedar betrayed as real sorrow as a man may feel for a tree".[15]

Sir Edward's interest in science, sustained since boyhood through all the long busy years in London, continued as acute as ever. Mosses became his special study; he loved them both for "their delicate beauty and the biological questions they aroused"[13]. He found them in Failand and sought them on his travels, taking out his pocket microscope whenever he found a promising stone or piece of an old wall.

He had relinquished his distinguished position as a High Court Judge without a qualm. To keep his hand in, and with no sense of diminution of his dignity, he undertook the chairmanship of Somerset Quarter Sessions. He sat too on the County Council, giving them the benefit of his legal knowledge. Once, in the matter of a disputed right of way in his own area of Failand, he not only gave his professional opinion but walked the entire

---

[14] Some busts were still in place in the 1960s when Mr. & Mrs. P. Robinson lives at Failand House.
[15] *Sir Edward Fry* op. cit.

length of the footpath in the hot summer sun (He was by then eighty-three).

So from the very beginning of his retirement Sir Edward was occupied to the full. He had an abundance of interests in his own home, and continued contact with his old world of the law. For his daughters and his wife the transition to the new life cannot have been so easy. When they first came down to live permanently at Failand, Margery could not escape a "feeling of panic" at being immersed in the tiny inaccessible hamlet through the "soft sad winters of the Bristol Channel". Soon after the family settled in she was allowed to go to Somerville College Oxford for two years (she did not take a degree), but returned home again with a great sense of desolation. Her brother Roger, to whom she was very close, warned her of what would be the depressing, enervating effect for her of the anxious, unnecessary fussing over minor ailments, the discouragement of any slightly risky undertaking, what Roger called the "invalidism" at Failand. She need not have worried. She was soon up and away, first as librarian of her old college and on then to a distinguished career — penal reformer, Principal of Somerville, friend of great men and women. Once she had made the break she delighted in coming back home to visit her family as often as she could.

Mariabella, Joan, Agnes and Ruth were permanently at home, and gradually developed their relationship with the village. Very soon after the family's arrival these young women set out bravely, since they felt they should begin as they meant to go on, to visit their father's tenants. As they talked at lunch, on their return, "they found they had severally visited the same cottage in the course of the morning; the object of their visits had kept a careful silence, sensing the predicament of these ardent young women with little to do"[16]. It must have been about now that the Frys began to employ local help, indoors and out, for there are families in Failand whose grandparents were coachmen, gardeners, estate carpenters, maids and housekeepers at Failand House. This, rather than self-conscious visiting of the sick or elderly, probably did much to strengthen the bonds with the village people. The little grand-daughter of one of Sir Edward's head gardeners was named Agnes and photographed sitting on Lady Fry's lap.

She still lives in Failand today in the house where her grandparents lived before her, and she remembers that she was considered to be one of Miss Agnes' favourites. Although they were not known as generous employers as far as wages were concerned, the Frys had a well-developed and endearing sense of occasion; they always gave presents, some of them very

---

[16] from *Margery Fry* by Enid Huw Jones.

handsome, both at Christmas and to commemorate weddings, births, golden weddings and retirements. One may go into houses in Failand still and see splendid twelve-piece tea sets arranged in pristine condition on sitting-room shelves, substantial clocks, trays, sets of knives and forks, all handed down to succeeding generations.

On the golden wedding day of one old couple, the Emerys, who lived in the first pair of cottages[17] along Failand Lane, the Frys came down in the carriage, complete with footmen, and presented every member of the family with a little drawstring bag containing a golden sovereign. These bags are still treasured by the Emery's descendants, now scattered far and wide. The year was probably 1908 (just before Sir Edward and Lady Fry celebrated their own golden wedding). The Emery family group was photographed, their chairs ranged right across the lane outside their front gate, the same lane down which the Frys drove to the Quaker Meeting at Portishead on Sundays. One can see grass growing down the middle of it, so probably the photographer was not disturbed at his work.

Perhaps the Frys came into closest touch with their tenants and the village as a whole through the Schoolroom. The private pioneering of adult education was often undertaken by Quakers living in the country. Sir Edward, with his great love of learning and a ready made supply of eager instructresses, decided to erect a small detached building where people could come and be taught all manner of extra-mural activities, and Failand people seem wholeheartedly to have enjoyed themselves here. Music was taught by Mariabella and there was a band of wind and stringed instruments. There was plenty of instruction in basketwork and embroidery. Some pieces of needlework undertaken in the nineteen hundreds under the Frys' tuition are still carefully kept and occasionally brought out to admire. Their strong, deep colours and bold frieze patterns are quite unlike the usual sentimental designs of Edwardian fancywork. Margery's influence would appear to have been at work here. There is an account in her biography of her involvement with Quaker relief organisations in Europe during the First World War. She experimented in teaching the refugees a new kind of embroidery. "In her spare moments Margery began to devise patterns: doodles on squared paper still fall from the pages of her notebooks. She filled in geometric designs with bright wools worked on coarse linen or calico"[18]. Richly coloured wools from the craft workshop, the Omega, started by Roger in London, were obtained by Ruth and sent out to her sister in France. The designs upon the finished pieces of embroidery were subsequently admired in London as very "avant garde". No doubt similar patterns and wools found their way to Failand, and this

---

[17] now Stone Cottage.
[18] *Margery Fry* opus cit.

would account for the exceptional and striking work done at the village classes. Some articles still in existence were made by an old lady when she was a very young girl in domestic service (not with the Frys) — she attended the classes on her day off.

Astronomy, always an interest of Lady Fry, was also taught; there are those in the village today who remember being led out onto the roof of Failand House to observe an eclipse through smoked glass, and there was a telescope, though only the boys were allowed to use it. The girls, indignant at this unfair distinction, took their revenge by punching holes in the boys' leatherwork while they were away under instruction with the instrument. There was bad blood also between youngsters coming up from nearby Pill (Miss Agnes taught Botany at Pill school), and on one occasion the Failand youngsters hid in a barn and pelted the 'intruders' with potatoes. While the main beneficiaries of the classes were adults and youngsters who had left school, there was also entertainment for the young children. This often took the form of magic lantern shows. The same slides tended to re-appear and then the audience grew fidgety and bored, escaping thankfully when permission was given to run out and gather up the fallen mulberries on the lawn outside.

At Easter time, Easter Egg hunts were organised for the children in the grounds of Failand House. The silver papered eggs, properly numbered, were hidden about the shrubbery, and every child had to look for the egg with his or her number on. This sensible idea was sometimes thrown into chaos by one naughty boy, his name still not forgotten, who simply ate each egg as he found it, and pushed the silver papers into his trouser pocket. Even after she had moved away from Failand, Miss Agnes occasionally returned to organise an Egg Hunt, this time in the grounds of the Chantry, where she used to stay with the Curate and his family.

As far as the village school was concerned, it is still clearly remembered that Miss Agnes, though she had no official position there, went in and out of it as of right. She was a wonderful botanist, and knowing the name of every local flower and plant she made a book of them for the children which was still in the school's possession when it closed in 1985. There is an excellent story of her in her later years, standing in front of a class to demonstrate the strange behaviour of the South American diving spider. This insect lived below the surface of the water in an air-bubble. Calling in her deep voice for a glass of water from the kitchen Agnes plunged in her finger, woollen glove and all, with a most impressive result, since her gloved finger obligingly swelled up, mimicking the habit of the strange creature. Agnes also procured for the school a charming mural showing the adventures of Peter Rabbit, painted by Roger. This remained on the walls for some time until it was needed for an exhibition, when it was removed.

In the early days of Sir Edward's retirement Mariabella was much at

Weston-Super-Mare helping to nurse Portsmouth, but her training later brought her into especially close touch with the local people. Her parents bought a donkey cart so that she might easily get about the neighbourhood nursing the sick and helping to deliver the babies. She was extremely smartly turned out in her uniform and, as the years passed, became somewhat forbidding in her demeanour. She certainly took cases as far out as Long Ashton for there she brought into the world the baby girl who, as a young woman attended the Fry embroidery classes as we have heard, and who into her old age would still speak affectionately of "Miss Mabs".

Mariabella and Agnes always remained at Failand, Joan and Ruth were often absent as they grew older. Before the First War, Joan went to Guildford to look after Roger's children; their mother's severe mental illness had brought domestic tragedy into his life. Joan returned for a while to Failand but her work for the Quakers took her increasingly away from home. After the war she settled in London. Ruth, delicate though she was, journeyed extensively over Europe during the war years as the Secretary of the Friends' War Victims Relief organization. All this time, Agnes, with Mariabella, held the fort at Failand, Agnes economising with relish when food was short, watching the rosebeds turned over to growing cabbages, sending parcels of beautifully made garments to her sister's refugees in France, and writing to them the kind of letters that made them think lovingly of the family at Failand.

And what of Lady Fry as her daughters grew into middle age, each developing her own interests and all except Agnes and Mariabella leaving home at last? The generation of village people who really knew her is gone. There is a brief remembered glimpse of her coming out onto the lawn in the nineteen twenties to watch the Easter Egg Hunt, dressed in an earlier fashion, her black skirt touching the ground, a little black cap upon her head. Her generosity is recalled, for she and Agnes arranged the fostering in their cottages and farms of many poor children from South Wales. Her Quaker abhorrence of strong drink was absolute. She and Sir Edward had early put an official stop to the manufacture and sale of cider on their farms and the story is told of how she sent for and severely rebuked the wife of one of her servants, who, after suffering a slight accident, was taken into the Failand Inn and restored with a very small tot of brandy. The Frys liked their tenants to attend temperance meetings, and if possible to 'sign the pledge'.

These are external impressions. Perhaps only her immediate family knew Lady Fry as she really was. Her function in welding her family together was recognized by all of them. "How your wonderful power of sympathy and interest in all our doings does help us. I often, when I feel I can't go on caring about other people's affairs, wonder how you do it", wrote Margery. Yet in a family where so many practical successes were earned, so much intellectual enthusiasm generated, Lady Fry seems somehow to have failed to use her talents, to have frittered away her long life dealing with the endless minutiae of running her household. We do get one glimpse of the charming and efficient hostess she could have been if she had so wished. In 1908 Sir Edward, already experienced in the work of industrial tribunals, was called upon to act as arbitrator in an international dispute between France and Germany[19]. This necessitated taking up residence for weeks at a time at the Hague — it is remembered in Failand that the Frys even shipped out their grand piano, for the rest of the family went out there from time to time to stay. In a letter of Margery's we have a picture of Lady Fry in very unusual company and plainly glorying in it. "We are a very odd party here[20], and perhaps the quaintest of all is to see Mother, a very piquant mixture of her usual self with a quite new personality out of that store of unused selves which she has even more than most people. It was really worth eating through a long dinner ... to see her acting as host to the old Turk, a great beau of hers, just as it was somewhat startling to see Father gallantly lighting the cigar of an Ambassador" (Sir Edward abominated tobacco). Perhaps it was her long and plainly most happy marriage which was Lady Fry's real achievement. Even Isabel, who found her mother so difficult to get on with, recognised the complete harmony which existed between her parents.

Sir Edward lived on through the First War but by 1916 his health had begun to fail; Margery, anxious about him, sent a postcard every day from Switzerland. Yet a year later Roger was astonished at his vitality. "My father has just worked out with me a most admirable letter on the Pope's peace proposals." When, in October 1918, death came, it was mercifully swift. For Roger, who had always loved his father dearly, in spite of their differences, "it was infinitely quicker and better than I feared." He wrote that sentence as he sat in Failand Churchyard. His father had been buried in as yet unconsecrated ground, the rough meadowland which surrounded the church[21]. If that had not been possible, Lady Fry would have laid him to rest in the grounds of his own beloved house. She herself, old and grieving, sat in a chair in the vestry by the open door from where she could see the committal service.

Two years later died Mariabella, at the early age for a Fry of 59. She lies beside her parents, the only other member of the family buried in the churchyard. Lady Fry lived on another twelve years after her husband's death. Apparently, her way of life changed little, though she exchanged

---

[19] The Casa Blanca Incident.
[20] Indeed the Fry daughters visiting their parents at the Hague 'en bloc' are described by one observer as "an extraordinary group".
[21] Church built 1887; churchyard consecrated 1919: church consecrated 1924.

her carriage for a stately motor car, never allowed to go at more than twenty miles an hour. Yet, in these last years after her husband's death, she seems to have opened out in the glow of a late, Indian Summer, into a warmer, happier, more mellow character altogether. There was a significant development in her relationship with her son Roger. Now, suddenly, he felt very close to her and she responded to him, old as she was, in a way which surprised and moved him. "It is not to be believed how much she's changed . . . It shows what a portentous pressure my father exercised over her", he wrote. He could talk to her about anything and was delighted by her wit. To this time of ease must belong the local memory of Roger, hatless and casually dressed as if he were among his own Bloomsbury friends, ready to chat to anyone he might meet in the Failand lanes or in the bar of the Inn — that same public house of which his mother had so strongly disapproved in years gone by.

Margery was often at home with her mother in these last years. They enjoyed each other's company more than ever; they were as close now as mother and daughter could be. Margery would read aloud from the newspaper, amusing Lady Fry with her wicked and informed comments upon her contemporaries, poking fun too at herself, distinguished as she was in the world outside. Her mother sat at Failand in 1928 and listened as Margery made her first wireless broadcast.

On the afternoon of her death, a Wednesday afternoon in March 1930, it is still remembered in Failand that Lady Fry, ninety-seven years old by now, took a nap in the orchid house. Sir Edward had always loved orchids and in London days he used to show off his special treasures to the family, every Sunday. It was their rich profusion that he gloried in — one Isabel remembered as a "great waterfall of white and gold" — and there had always been an orchid house at Failand. No doubt on a chilly March afternoon its fragrant warmth made it an ideal place for an old lady to sleep.

In the evening she sat reading a new book on astronomy, always her subject. It was Sir James Jeans' *The Universe Around Us*. She was enjoying it and she recommended it to Margery, who was with her. A few hours later, quickly and easily, she died. Exactly a week later there died in Failand another old lady. Lady Fry had for a number of years sent down to her soup from the kitchen, always on a Wednesday. The gentle little joke went round the village, that the old lady had died because, this Wednesday, the mistress being dead, there was no soup.

Now only Agnes was left at home. Immediately after mother's death she made a trip with Margery to British Columbia. She came back to the great empty house and stayed alone in it until about 1936. She continued in all her many works with characteristic vigour, and so we see her, absolutely herself, assisting at the ceremonial planting of the Jubilee Oak. Soon afterwards she left Failand House for Brent Knoll where she resettled herself in a house called Orchard View. In her latter years her character lost none of its unique flavour. She often asked people from Failand to pay her a visit. One such memorable one was made by the village schoolmistress who, after changing at school into a suitable dress, drove down the main Bridgwater Road in a torrential thunderstorm, bidden to an evening meal with Miss Agnes. "You're late", Miss Fry pronounced, as Miss Cooke and her friend struggled in out of the downpour. Small talk was never easy with Agnes but the sudden death in Oxhouse Lane of a well-known inhabitant of Failand kept the conversation going. Then the party gathered round the enormous and beautiful oval dining table. There were six of them in all including a lady's maid from the old days. A large tray of tea was placed upon the table followed by a gigantic platter with a domed silver cover. The cover was lifted to reveal fourteen chipolata sausages, symmetrically arranged, each one backed by a single croquette potato. "You serve, Miss Cooke." Each person received two sausages, but the two travellers from Failand had an extra one each to fortify them after their unpleasant journey. Miss Cooke, very young and inexperienced, managed somehow the ordeal of distribution. Some cold gooseberries and somewhat hard sponge-fingers completed the repast. The lady's maid and her friend escaped to the kitchen but the rest were obliged to turn their minds to possible entertainment. "Magic lantern?" said Miss Fry hopefully. There was no immediate response. "Paper folding?" No one demurred, and the rest of the evening passed in a demonstration of origami. It seems somehow satisfying to take leave of the family with this little story. For all their quirks and eccentricities, their sometimes over-serious concentration upon instruction, education and moral rectitude, the Frys were good people with good intentions towards those among whom they lived so long. Talk about them will often raise a smile but it is an affectionate one. Whatever your mistakes and failures you are judged hereabouts in the end by what you have "done" for Failand. The Frys did much, and they set the seal upon their doing with their final action; in remembrance of Edward and Mariabella, the family gave to the National Trust and so to Failand all their fair acres, meadows, oak woods, uplands and streams, a magnificent inheritance of exceptional grace and beauty.

What follows, still under the heading of "The Frys of Failand", is included partly because it gives a further insight into the character of Lady Fry but chiefly to save from oblivion a crystal clear account of the small detail of a child's life in the early nineteenth century. Mariabella Fry was well over ninety when she set down her early memories in 1927 and they are all the more remarkable for that. Ackworth, which she mentions, must have been her family's country home. Bruce Grove, also named, was probably their London house; she was born in Tottenham.

When I was a Little Child

I. THINGS THAT WERE NOT.

Lucifer matches.
Railway trains (until I was 7 or 8 years old).
Gas-lights.
Cabs.
Steam-printing.
Photographs.
Gutta-percha.
Omnibuses.
Policemen.
Postage stamps.
Hot-water bottles.
Night-lights.
Christmas Trees.
India-rubber goods.
Goloshes.
Bicycles.

Telegrams.
Perambulators.
Hoardings with posters.
Lawn tennis.
Safety pins.
Clinical thermometers.
Electro-plate.
Japanese anemones.
Crinolines.
Spring mattresses.
Eiderdowns.
Anaesthetics.
Gas for teeth extraction.
Sewing machines.
Carbolic disinfectants.
Aniline dyes.

II. THINGS THAT WERE.

Flint and steel.
Rushlights.
Hackney coaches.
Mail coaches with four horses.
Large easy carriages with C springs and steps to let down.
Warming pans.
Hand-coloured prints.

Medicines:

"Prunes and senna."
Almond emulsion.
Manna.

Watchmen at night.

Sweets:

Confits and goats' eggs.
Hundreds & thousands.

Sweeps on May day and Jack in the Green.
Flails.
Clogs and pattens.
Beadles.
Chariots.
Poplin.
Bonnet-caps.
Bat, trap and ball.
Four-penny pieces.
Guineas.
Hatchments.
Bath-houses (out of doors)
Watches in fobs.
Watch-cases.
Tippets and sleeves (in one).
Daguerreotypes (just beginning).
Naphtha lamps.
Snuff boxes.
Chartists.

COMMENTS.

Lucifer Matches When I was a little child, the fires were either kept alight all night, or lit with flint and steel. I remember a tinder-box, with tinder in it, but don't think I saw it used. We had rush-lights which kept burning all night at Ackworth.

Railways I remember the first time I travelled by train. I believe it was the year 1840. We were returning from our usual stay at Ackworth, and the railway was then opened as far north as Rugby. So we travelled (by coach or post-chaise — I forget which) to Rugby, and then got into a carriage much like the usual coach, and by and bye, it began to move slowly, and the elders began remarking, "Why, it doesn't move faster than a post-chaise." Nothing more remains in my mind, but I have a dim recollection in after journeys, of helping, as I thought it, to drag a heavy carpet-bag about, because there were no people like porters to look after the luggage.

Gas-lights Of course there were no gas-lights either in streets or houses. The Grove, Bruce Grove, was lighted by naphtha lamps, managed, of course, by a lamp-lighter, and up to about the time when I was born, a watch-man used to walk up and down all night, crying occasionally, "Past one o'clock and a cold, frosty morning!" or whatever the time and weather might be. I even heard of his shouting a message to my grandmother about some illness in our house.

Cabs Instead of cabs, there were some rather musty "hackney-coaches," and ordinary coaches, which plied like omnibuses. My father when he did not ride on horse-back, would engage a place in "Winder's coach."

Goloshes I have said there were no goloshes, but I remember some strange, thick, clumsy shoes made of india-rubber for men. Of course, Bessie and I had wooden clogs, or pattens, with hinged soles, I believe. We liked pattering about in clogs.

Sweeps and May-day The little chimney-sweeps had a holiday on May-day, and they went round to the houses of well-to-do people, dressed up with green leaves, etc., asking for charity; other children, too, went about with bunches of flowers and greenery, singing, or rather shouting, as nearly as I recollect, the following rhyme:—

> "Good people all, I come to you
>   Upon the first of May,
> I have been gathering all the night,
>   And great part of the day,
> And now I have returned back,
>   I've brought you a bunch of May.
> A branch of May to you I've brought,
>   Before your door it stands,
>   'Tis but a sprout,
>   'Tis all budded out,
>   The work of Our Lord's hands.
>   Please remember the garland!"

Flails I well remember the sound of the flail in my grandfathers farm at Ackworth. It seemed to go on all day — and sometimes we saw the winnowing, but not often. The farm-yard with the great pigeon house was a great attraction, but it was rather forbidden ground, except when we rode up and down by turns on the donkey, longing for cross old Simon, the gardener, to come behind, as he *sometimes* did, with a stick and very loud exclamations, and made the creature scamper along a few yards. This donkey we harnessed to a green, wooden cart, the only representative of a "pram" in those days, and made him drag us about (if he would). We used to stand upon his back to pick Siberian crabs of which we were fond. (But this is all a digression.)

Anaesthetics Of course, there was no chloroform for operations. As a girl, I heard of another girl (who afterwards became a great friend of mine) who had to have one of her toes amputated, and I was told of the great heroism with which she bore the pain: *I think*, without even groaning. A few years ago, my friend, Lady Paget, told me that when she first married, Dr. Paget, as he then was, had to live in a house close to the Hospital, and on operation days she could hardly bear to stay at home and hear the awful screams of the patients.

Warming-pans I do not think that hot water bottles (water babies), came in till about the fifties, though, of course, there were stone ones. But warming-pans were in continued use. I can see the chambermaid in one of the Inns (they were not "Hotels" then), warming the bed in which I was to sleep, and oh! the joy of that wide-spread heat. But it was short-lived, for the sheets soon got cold again.

Medicines I have given some of the favourite medicines of our childhood. No doubt many of the present drugs were in use. I think we were a good deal doctored in our childhood, perhaps from having a physician in "Uncle Doctor." There was a good deal more tuberculosis in those days — it was called "consumption," and we often heard of a "galloping consumption." Often one in a family died of it, and I can count several families of our friends and acquaintances in which this was the case; in one family of eight, five died during my youth. Death was much impressed upon us, and we were sometimes taken to see people after they were dead — a most objectionable practice. We were on the whole healthy, but I was considered very delicate, as I had inflammation of the lungs once at least, when I was about four. On this occasion a kind Uncle brought me a box of lovely tea-things (I have them still), and brought them up to me as I sat in my crib. Though no doubt longing to have them, I resolutely and firmly shut my eyes, and in spite of cajolements and commands, refused to open them. My Uncle departed, the tea-things were no doubt taken away, and I was left under the ban of displeasure. This was one of those secret inhibitions which are a part of childhood, and arise probably from vehement shyness. Until I was seven years old, when I had the scarlet fever, I was, I remember, often called "the little invalid," a title which highly incensed me. I was made to wear warmer clothes, and long trousers. But after the scarlet fever, I became strong and healthy; of course, during my illness I was kept apart in the nursery, and the others were not allowed to come upstairs, but when I was getting better, they all came half-way up to look at me as I stood on the landing, and received me with hilarious joy. I simply burst into tears. Some time after this,

"Tommy" had the whooping cough, called by my grandfather the "Ching cough" (an old word), and after we had caught it and were well again, we were sent to Gravesend to recuperate, and there had the delight of witnessing a real Guy Fawkes day. Squibs and crackers thrown up at windows, a big tar barrel rolled alight down the steep street, and no doubt Guy was burned, but him I don't remember.

Tea   Tea, of course, was much scarcer and dearer formerly, and the poor were very glad of tea leaves. One or two women used to come regularly to our house for our used tea leaves, with which, by pouring boiling water on them, they made a drink *called* tea, which must have been mostly tannin.

Postage   Letters used to be folded in a sheet of paper, like a parcel, and sealed carefully (no gummed envelopes, of course). Often they had a large 2 on them to signify, I believe, that they had come by the 2d. post, which took letters in the London area for that sum. But sometimes they had a signature outside of some Member of Parliament, of either House, which was called a "frank." Every Member could give or use one "frank" a day, which meant he could write his name on the outside of the letter, which then required no postage but went free. As my father and uncle knew many such individuals, they often were able to send letters free, and often a letter would begin, "As I have a 'frank' to-day, I will send you word that" so-and-so. If there was no "frank" the letter had a figure on it, 8d., or 10d., or 1s. as the case might be, and the postman would not deliver the letter till that was paid. Often in stories of the time, a poor family receives a letter, possibly a gift of money, which was out of their reach because they could not pay the postage.

The penny post came in, I think, in 1840, and the curious papers for enfolding them caused great excitement and amusement, but they soon gave way to stamped envelopes, and, after, to stamps.

MARIABELLA FRY,
Written in 1927.

Chapel and Church

Failand springs one magnificent architectural surprise; no stranger following the narrow lanes down from the main road to Clevedon towards Portbury is prepared for the sudden sight of a vast neo-Gothic church with a great east window, a spire 120 feet high and a mighty vicarage on the same gargantuan scale in tow. How it came to be there, stately among the muddy fields, is an interesting story.

Until the early nineteenth century the people of Failand were expected to attend church, to be married and buried in Wraxall. How many of them troubled to make the journey down there we do not know, but probably only a handful of people who lived up the 'top end'. Down the bottom end of the hamlet there appeared in 1825 a small Wesleyan Methodist chapel. It was built on the side of the lane just past Failand House, opposite the Home Farm. It continued to find support, chiefly from the people of Lower Failand, for over a century, handy and cosy as it was. One family, the Willmotts[1], filled the chapel in its later years almost unaided. Eddie, who was at one time gardener to the Fry family, lived in Rambler Cottage, very near by, and he had fifteen children; together with friends and relations they formed a congregation on their own. In its isolation the little chapel was probably run by a lay preacher, or at least a locally based man, and no doubt the simple service, with lessons, extempore prayers, hymns and sermon, went down well. Perhaps this state of affairs pushed the church at Wraxall into action. On September 8th, 1845 the Bishop of Bath and Wells issued a 'licence for Divine Service in the Schoolroom at Failand'. As we have already seen this schoolroom had been established in Failand in 1839 to teach local children, and was later incorporated into the school buildings proper. The reason given for the new arrangement is that 'the inhabitants of the hamlet . . . are residing at a distance from the Parish Church which makes their attendance in many cases inconvenient . . . There is a place within the said hamlet called and known as the Schoolroom, which may be fitted up and made convenient for the celebration of Divine Service there'. The Bishop grants his licence 'for the time being', so that Failand people can 'assemble in the said schoolroom for the celebration of Divine Service therein, according to the Rites and

---

[1] This name first appears in Wraxall Church Register in 1580.

Ceremonies of the United Church of England and Ireland as it is now by Law established'.

So for the next forty years matters continued thus in Failand. You went to chapel or you went to the makeshift church in the schoolroom. Meanwhile down in Wraxall the Vaughan family had established itself at the Rectory. James Vaughan had been inducted as Rector there in 1801. His wife Sarah bore him three sons, Richard, James and Edward Protheroe. Edward, in the fullness of time — 1857 — became Rector. His brother Richard, plainly a man of substance, was settled in a very comfortable way on the outskirts of Bath. When the idea of giving Failand a proper church of its own arose we do not know, but Richard Vaughan made the church a gift to the Rectory of Wraxall, linked indissolubly with it, and this apparently without any prior consultation with the Diocesan authorities. It represented an excellent living for his nephew Henry, son of Edward Protheroe Vaughan. The curate's stipend — it was a curacy — was a generous one, £800 per year. In 1887, when the church was built, this represented a handsome sum of money, the envy of many other clergyman in Somerset. The house which went with the living, the Chantry, was large and dignified, set about with stained glass, its main staircase wide and handsome. A solid detached stable block was soon added, to accommodate the carriages and horses of the new incumbent. The land for church and Chantry was purchased from the Gibbs family at Wraxall. The whole outlay for land and buildings was some £12,000. The stipend of £800 per annum was guaranteed by an endowment made by Richard Vaughan and known as the Vaughan Trust.

All this great enterprise was undertaken in the mistaken belief that the splendid new church was set just where a new main road would come through, linking Bristol, Portishead and Clevedon. It would, so the Vaughans believed, soon serve the thriving community which would grow up there. Instead it was the top road from Bristol to Clevedon, as we have it now, which was metalled, in 1895, and the development when it came was in Upper Failand, along this new modern road. The great church stands isolated among the fields today just as it did in 1887. Only the pine trees, small and unobtrusive a hundred years ago when they were set round St. Bartholomew's, have increased in size till they darken the church and must be lopped back where they overhang the narrow lane.

No-one who attended the opening of the church on the April evening in 1887 would have been thinking along these lines. The church could seat three hundred; forty people had taken communion on the morning of April 17th and no doubt there was a full house for the ceremonial service in the evening. The new curate, Henry Vaughan, read the prayers and preached his first sermon in his new church. His father, Edward, gave the final blessing. Sir Edward Fry, not yet retired from the Bench but already resident for ten years in Failand House with his family, read the lesson. Quaker though he was he seems to have had no objection to taking part in such an important local event in an Anglican church. His love for Failand as we shall see later was strong indeed and he would not have hesitated to be a part of the place at such a great moment in its history.

As many a parson knows to his cost, his congregation at set piece gatherings melts away like snow in summer once the regular routine of humdrum services is all that is on offer. The church at its inception served not more than a hundred or so people. There was already a strong loyalty to the Methodist chapel, and we know that with untroubled conscience more than one inhabitant of the hamlet went to chapel in the morning and church at night. The great building with its high pitched roof and vast size, buffetted often by all the winds that blow, was, as it still is, a greedy consumer of heat to very little purpose. Halfway up each side of the huge west window, on the inside, you can still see two hooks to hold the thick heavy curtain with which it was partially covered in winter, in an attempt to mitigate the effects of the cold. The coalburning boiler in the basement heated hot pipes and later radiators, but the wind whistled round the lectern unrestrained. Lighting was provided by the oil lamps; the chains which supported them can still be seen, and they were still being used by the Second World War. Electricity arrived in Failand a few years later. The single bell, damaged at Wraxall when a pinnacle fell from the tower, was installed in the tower of St. Bartholomew's in 1893, but it tolled for no funerals until 1919 when the churchyard was at last consecrated. It greeted no bride until 1920, when permission was at last granted for the solemnization of matrimony in the church. Until the 1960s it was still supposed that the church itself had never been consecrated. The Vaughans it will be remembered had put up the church at Failand without properly consulting the Diocesan authority. In fact, it was tardily discovered, the church was consecrated in 1924, which proved to be a mixed blessing. It now became subject to a quinquennial architectural survey and its congregation liable to keep the extensive fabric in repair.

With all the problems presented by its upkeep and the disadvantage of its position so far from the main centre of population it would have surprised no one if Failand Church had been unable to survive. Contrary to expectation and gloomy forecast however St Bartholomew's stands in full use today, re-roofed and in good repair and preparing, in 1987 to celebrate its centenary. In 1978 it was decided by the Diocesan authority at Bath and Wells that Failand no longer warranted a curate of its own; it must share the Rector with Wraxall, the mother church, though it would still benefit from the Vaughan Trust which had financed it from the beginning. The Chantry, the curate's house, had already been sold and replaced with a modern 'little' Chantry, in the new Sixty Acre development in Upper

Failand; it had seemed sensible to place the parson where the bulk of his flock was now to be found. When Failand lost its curate the Little Chantry was sold and the money invested.

There is no doubt that the loss of their own parson was felt by the true hamlet people. They could remember when it had been a privilege to share one's piece of bread and cheese and perhaps a home grown tomato with 'parson' as he came visiting, and they respected those of their curates who took off their jackets, called for a spade and gave a hand to anyone busy in their garden when they had called. Changes must come however and it was something that Failand still had a church of its own. Regular worshippers or not, Failand people still hold theirs in great affection and pray for its continued solid presence among them.

Failand School in the Twentieth Century

Memories of schooldays in the hamlet reach back through mothers and grandmothers to the earliest decades of the new century. Things were probably very little different from the end of Queen Victoria's reign; the local school was still the place where the children of local farm labourers and other humble people sent their children. If there was a lot of work to be done in the fields then the children were kept at home to help, and to try and prevent this the school authorities gave incentives to encourage regular attendance. One reward for a whole year without absence was a new pair of boots. There were some families where there was real hardship and the quiet generosity of the Vaughan family of Wraxall sometimes provided unobtrusive help for those who needed it. It is remembered that the schoolchildren in those days were expected to acknowledge the carriages of the gentry as they passed along the lanes. The Frys especially expected a curtsey from the girls and a salute with the hand to the forehead from the boys. If such acknowledgement was not forthcoming the headmistress would hear about it and the children would receive a reprimand. Knowing the Frys, who always had the moral welfare of their tenants at heart, it would have been their concern not that they themselves had been slighted but that the children should be well-behaved for their own good, according to the custom of the time. The family's connection with the school and lively interest in its progress was at the heart of the matter.

During these early years of the twentieth century, the tiny little schoolhouse somehow managed to provide living accommodation not only for the headmistress but often for her growing family. The head during the First World War was a Mrs. Hicks who was married to a groom at Tyntesfield, Lord Wraxall's place over the hill. Mr. Hicks spent the war as batman to one of the Gibbs[1] family, but his wife reared four children in the cramped quarters of the schoolhouse, as well as running the school. One of these children was 'put out' at three weeks old to be minded by her aunt nearby in the hamlet, and remained in her comfortable house to be brought up. With such happy, easy-going arrangements did people relieve their domestic problems in those uninhibited times.

---

[1] Lord Wraxall's family name.

In the nineteen twenties we find the first entries in the school register of children who lived in the new houses beginning to appear on the flat fields of Upper Failand, in the area now known as Sixty Acres. In its beginning this development was referred to somewhat scornfully by the indigenous population of the hamlet as "tin town"; many of the early bungalows were made of corrugated iron. Until now the higher part of the hamlet had been as sparsely populated as its lower reaches. One or two big farms, the Failand Inn, Failand Lodge and the small number of cottages and houses grouped about the Longwood cross-roads were all its dwellings. Gipsies often camped on the verges up there, carving pegs to sell in Bristol and helping themselves to chickens and the water from the outside rainwater tanks which stood in nearby gardens. The occasional market cart, the Frys' chocolate coloured carriage, or a horsedrawn brake on an expedition to the seaside were all that passed that way. Then gradually the twentieth century began to set its characteristic stamp on the place. House names like 'Kia-Ora' and 'Sundown' begin to crop up in the Failand School register and by the late 1930s the numbers of children at the school who came from 'top' Failand had greatly increased. The country children became acquainted with a different kind of life; the little, still sheltered community took a further step into the outside world.

We are lucky to have a first hand account of the working of the school during the years leading up to the Second World War. The author is Miss Poole, who still lives not far away.

"I was apppointed as Infant Teacher at Failand School on September 2nd 1930. I lodged at a house in the village where I paid the princely sum of fifteen shillings a week for full board and lodging, which included my laundry. My landlady was a wonderful person whose kindness and care almost overwhelmed me. The School House was occupied by Miss Grigg, the Headmistress and her family . . . The School building was not very large, just two classrooms. We had no water on the premises; it had to be carried from a tap in a spring some distance from the school. There was one rainwater tank that supplied water for two washbasins and the primitive toilets. For many years there were sixty children on the roll, aged from five to fourteen years.

Dinners were supplied for the whole school at the cost of one penny for the main meal, and a halfpenny for the pudding. The cooking was done everyday by Miss Grigg's mother and sisters in the schoolhouse. (The same little house where Mrs. Hicks had raised her family. How did they manage to cook there for some sixty children?). The menu . . . included stews, pies, salads and roasts. Parents occasionally sent vegetables or fruit, and the lady at Failand House (Miss Agnes Fry) sometimes sent a rabbit, or bones for stews. The senior girls did the washing up, supervised by the teacher on duty. Failand was the only school in Somerset to provide hot lunch for the pupils. Most of the pupils lived fairly near the school, a few coming from another part of Failand where the houses were few and far between (Sixty Acre). Some of the children walked about three miles to school in all weathers and consequently in the Winter wet coats and shoes were always drying round the two open fires and the Tortoise stove.

In the classroom there was a huge trunk containing clothes for dressing up. We could find almost any costume we needed for a play. Miss Grigg's father had been a docker so there had been no money to spare for extras when she was at school and that included costumes for the plays which her school had often put on. Miss Grigg was determined that no child at Failand school should suffer as she had, hence the wonderful trunk of fancy costumes. In 1932 most of Miss Grigg's family moved to Bristol, so the dinners were discontinued, but by this time milk was being supplied to all pupils at a halfpenny for a third of a pint . . .

In 1935 . . . the plan to send the older children to newly formed Senior Schools was . . . put into action . . . The Seniors were bussed daily to Pill. The Failand parents were very much against the transfer of the children to the next village, the residents there were so different from themselves . . . almost foreigners, most of the men at Pill being pilots, or having work in some way connected with boats."

After a few years, Miss Poole tells us, Failand forgot its differences with Pill, and all went smoothly. Another head took Miss Grigg's place, a Miss Grant, and she continued at Failand until the outbreak of war in 1939.

How cosy and attractive it all sounds:— open fires, with coats and shoes steaming gently beside the hearth, roast meat and rabbit stew, spring water to drink and all the excitement of rummaging in the dressing up trunk for the best costume you could put together for the play in hand. The war years, though, were drawing very close. How the little school fared under its new young head, Miss Dorothy Cooke, belongs with the last chapter, Failand at War.

The other house

A second family, beside the Frys, was a part of the life of the hamlet for nearly fifty years. Colonel and Mrs. Brittan inherited Failand Hill House in 1908 from the Colonel's aunt, who was the widow of a solicitor, Mr. Alfred Brittan. Mr. Brittan had bought the property from a Dr. Francis Black in 1876; the Doctor had built the house in 1871 on land belonging to the Blagrave family. The lane which runs past the house is still occasionally referred to locally as 'Brittan's Lane', and the Colonel well-remembered as the chairman for many years of the Failand Church Committee. Some who worked for the family still live not more than a few miles from Failand Hill. The house stands very close to the probable site of Medes Place; the old buttress, already noted as all that is left of that mediaeval dwelling, stands in grounds originally belonging to the Brittan estate. Failand Hill House is a dignified and solid building, beautifully proportioned and in an incomparable setting, and since much care has been lavished on it over the years it has kept its looks and its character.

The extra-mural embellishments of the Edwardian estate, however, have not worn so well. The magnificent vegetable garden with its splendid glasshouses, standing on the other side of the lane from the house is now quite run down behind its high wall. It no longer forms a part of the main property. The neat miniature farmhouse in pretty patterned brickwork with it separate circular dairy building is in disrepair. The bell in the tall tower which used to ring the estate workers in to their tasks in the morning and back from the fields at night rings no more. Anyone approaching the estate in the old days was admitted through the large white wooden gate at the Upper Lodge. The under chauffeur and his wife lived here and the chauffeur's wife ran out to open and shut the gate, often to let the Colonel's great Daimler in or out. You may still trace this way down. Upper Lodge, a charming cottage separate now from the estate, still bears its old name and the white gate still stands, though fast disintegrating.

Plenty of people still remember the self-contained little world of Failand Hill in times gone by. The atmosphere there must have differed sharply from that at Failand House. The Fry's establishment, eccentric, philanthropic, administered somewhat frugally though with the greatest kindness and goodwill, set an entirely different tone from the Brittan's, where matters seem to have been ordered in a more characteristically comfortable and easy fashion. In number it may be that the staff there was a more modest one than the Frys'. The Colonel employed a butler (the same for many years, a Mr. Lemon), an under-butler, cook, kitchenmaids, housemaids, houseboy, first chauffeur (the Colonel's batman in the 1914 war), second chauffeur, (the Colonel was an early motoring enthusiast), dairy maid and bailiff[1]. Yet the living was unmistakably more comfortable than in the Quaker household. There was a tennis court, a game room (the Colonel loved to shoot, always sending his retriever, Simple, to fetch his shooting boots), and a cricket pitch. This pitch had been presented to Failand by the Colonel's aunt and is still the Failand and Portbury Cricket Club ground. There was an annual Cricket Week in which W.G. Grace with his Failand connections sometimes took part, and the dinner of the club was held every year in Failand Hill House. Domestic wages here were considered to be generous where the Frys paid only adequately, and occasional treats were on a very satisfactory scale. The Colonel was a governor of Clifton Zoo and no-one ever forgot the day when he procured admittance for the whole of Failand School to the Zoological gardens, a lavish gesture in comparison with the small rewards handed out by the Frys. It says much for the good sense of local people that the genuine affection which they felt for the whole Fry family was in no way diminished by their thrifty habits.

The Colonel must have kept an excellent table. In addition to the plentiful supply of game, cream, eggs and butter came across from the little dairy every day. The head chauffeur's wife, who was in charge of the dairy, would arrange the produce most beautifully in a large flat basket, the butter shaped and embellished with patterns, sprigs of fresh parsley separating eggs and cream, and carry it across to the house herself; no-one else was allowed to touch it. The laundry, as in all the big houses in the neighbourhood, was sent out to be done by the cottagers. The great laundry cart pushed by the houseboy was a familiar sight in the lanes of Failand, fetching and carrying back the linen. Only Mrs. Brittan's high lace collars, two fresh ones each day, were washed at home. Her maid performed this little task, washing the collars in tea to keep their delicate colour and fragile beauty. Like Lady Fry, who always wore her skirts to the ground and a little lace cap until her death in 1930, the Colonel's wife seemed to care nothing for being in fashion. When she walked her retrievers every day on the high hills she always wore an old blue cloche hat, up to date in the 1920s but worn, like the lace collars, long after it was démodé. Mrs. Brittan, though a little formidable, was nevertheless liked and respected by her staff. She kept a kindly eye on the young ones; she had a few words with each of them when she paid them, which she did personally (and generously). Any of her maids who made a journey home or to friends on

---

[1] The estate workers were additional to these.

their days off were taken to the door of their destination, collected and brought safely back to Failand Hill. No-one was allowed to walk the lanes alone. Nonetheless, their mistress expected high standards of behaviour — one nurserymaid was reprimanded sharply for running across the road to the dairy without first putting on her coat.

As the years went by the staff diminished. It must have been the same story all over England as the 1930s wore on. Soon after the War, in 1949, the Colonel died, and the property passed on to his daughter and her husband, Colonel and Mrs. Chaytor. This couple was tragically killed in a motor accident and their two daughters soon afterwards left the hamlet. They still keep in touch, however, with some who served the family so long in Failand.

The market gardeners

Failand throughout most of the nineteenth century was so remote and self-sufficient that poachers felt quite safe to use its outlying farmhouses to drink in, out of reach of the Law. Cider was freely made and sold in those days at half a dozen or more of the farms in the hamlet; this was allowed by the Beerhouses Act of 1830. In the 1850s Mrs. Bunce of Lower Failand Farm, so her great-granddaughter used to tell, regularly hung a holly branch, a trail of ivy or other greenery over her front door to show in timehonoured fashion that drink was to be bought on the premises.[1] Her house was known locally and farther afield as 'The Bush House' and it was a favourite haunt of poachers who knew that rich rewards could be found in the woods and dingles of Failand. The police occasionally came looking for them, and since word of the constables' coming usually preceded them, the poachers had time to leg it over to Wales, leaving their snares and ferrets hidden at the farm. Granny Bunce took care of these until the coast was clear for them to come back and collect the tools of their trade. All such goings on were stopped when Lady Fry and her husband came to Failand House, in 1875. Quakers and rigid teetotallers, they liked their servants to 'sign the pledge' against the demon drink. There were no more alehouses in Failand, though cider continued to be made in the farms until well into the twentieth century.

In 1887 the great Church had come to throw its shadow over the lanes and fields of Lower Failand; the curate's was a regular sobering presence in the midst of the hamlet. In 1895 the rough wild road which ran across the ridge of top Failand was metalled, and no doubt the other roads into the city, down Beggar Bush Lane and along from Portishead to Clifton, steadily improved. The hamlet, no longer such a tight little community, was beginning to look more to the world outside, and in particular to the City of Bristol. In the 1880s and '90s, two or three Failand families had made their way into town with their market produce. By the early part of the new century, the trickle of carts had become a steady stream. Failand woke up fully to the fact that there was money to be made by supplying fresh fruit and vegetables, eggs and honey to the shops, schools and private houses of Clifton and Bristol, and with better roads they were ideally

---

[1] *Brewer's Dictionary of Phrase and Fable:* "an ivy-bush was once the common sign of taverns, and especially private houses where beer or wine could be obtained by travellers".

placed to take advantage of the situation. Some made it their sole livelihood, others augmented their wages as farm labourers or estate workers by joining in a small way with the bigger enterprises. The Smith family, who appear in the Wraxall Church Register of 1883 described as market gardeners, have been working the land in Lower Failand one way or another ever since. By the 1900s, they had under cultivation a sizeable piece of ground at the back of the dip in Oxhouse Lane, not far from where two members of the same family still farm, as tenants of the National Trust. The Potts are another family who appear early in the Church register described as market gardeners (1886), and their descendants were still making two trips a week into Bristol, on Tuesdays and Fridays, up to and into the Second World War. Mr. Mervyn Downs' grandfather, as we have seen, ran Failand Lodge as a market garden from the time he rented it from Lord Wraxall at the end of the nineteenth century; the Miss Balls of Upper Failand remembered him with his long beard sitting up behind his horses as his cart full of vegetables jogged across the Longwood Crossroads well before the 1914 war. Mr. Downs himself still takes his produce into Bristol — at least one Clifton greengrocer will offer you his cabbages 'fresh in this morning from Failand'. The Smiths, the Potts and the Downs are perhaps the best known and the first of the market gardeners but there were many more, especially during the 'Twenties and 'Thirties. Although Mr. Down is the only market garden left nowadays it is still possible if you look hard enough to find traces of the times when every available scrap of good land was put to use to grow produce of one kind or another. The best example of this is George Emery's Strip.

Walk down Failand Lane towards Portbury, past Jubbes Court and past Stone Cottage and you will notice, on the left-hand side where the trees begin to thicken, a strip of ground on the road-side of the hedge. It is raised; you have to scramble up on to it. It is quite wild now, and lately bluebells have begun to appear there in the spring. Some fifteen or twenty years ago you could still, if you were lucky, find a nice ripe William pear in the roadside grass, fallen from a very old tree which grew on the bank. (It was killed off at last, in the drought of 1970.) Local people generally strolled down at the right season to look for the fruit. A small blue plum and a greengage were further evidence of cultivation though they eventually fell victim to the crude slashing of a mechanical hedge-cutter. The piece of land where these old trees grew was once tended by the occupant of one half of what is now called Stone Cottage. His name was George Emery, the same George who with his wife Sarah received a bag of sovereigns from the Frys on the occasion of his golden wedding. George and Sarah lie together in Failand churchyard, but long after George's death in 1920, the name of his little extra garden lingered on; George Emery's Strip. As well as fruit he may have grown a rose or two there, for a beautiful single white rose of delicious scent appeared in the hedge opposite Stone Cottage every year until a few seasons ago. Mostly, however, George would have grown vegetables, and my guess is that he turned his hand to a bit of market gardening. He would have had room enough beside his cottage to grow the produce his family needed. The strip allowed him to branch out a little and make some extra money. Someone else would certainly have given him space on a cart going in to Bristol so transport would have been no problem.

Just opposite George's cottage at a little later date lived the Clark family. Mr. Clark had been a gardener at Failand Hill House, over the brow of the hill, and after he left there he had an arrangement with the head-gardener at the big house to take any unwanted produce from Colonel Brittan's walled garden there and sell it in Clifton. Mr. Clark too had a level high bank outside his property. The hedge still stands well back from the bank top, leaving a flat expanse of turf, and here he kept his beehives. The little girls and boys of Lower Failand in the 'Twenties and 'Thirties well remember the hives clustering beside the lane. The honey probably went into Bristol along with the garden produce.

The nearness of the hungry city to the fertile fields of Failand still imposes a pattern on what is grown hereabouts; potatoes for example for the dinner tables of Bristol. The owners of biggish gardens still sell off their surplus to nearby shops if they will pay a fair price, for there are one or two magnificent vegetable patches even now, whose owners grow well beyond their immediate need. They simply cannot help it; it is in their blood. There are plenty of memories of those busy days earlier in the century[2]. Someone's grandmother told her grandchildren how she sat up behind her father as they jogged on the cart down Beggar Bush Lane towards Clifton, shelling peas for dear life and throwing the shucks into the hedge. Probably a customer in town had asked for them ready prepared, a hotel, a club perhaps, or Clifton College. Milk had always gone in regularly to the College from Mulberry Farm on the edge of Failand; the school laundry was done here for many years, so there was a strong connection. And no-one forgets to tell you that if you wanted to bring your empty vegetable cart back from Bristol piled high with the succulent droppings from the well-fed horses of Clifton you must be back over the Bridge with your load by 8am, to avoid offending the nice noses of the ladies and gentlemen dwelling in that select district. Horse drawn vehicles continued to be used right up to the Second World War to bring in the market produce, and the

---

[2] There is a character in a novel entitled *Chatterton Square* by E.H. Young, who lives across the Bridge from Upper Radstowe (the author's name for Clifton) and who sells vegetables from his van to the householders in the residential squares. He seems to grow his produce on the borders of Abbots Leigh and Failand.

petrol shortage then prolonged the practice for a few more years. Nowadays the close link between Failand and the shops of Clifton and its immediate neighbourhood is all but broken. Bulk buying and economic change has seen to that. In their day though, the market gardeners of Failand must have given the people of Clifton and its neighbourhood a true, fresh taste of the real country.

The Flora of Failand

When you talk to people who knew our hamlet before the Second World War, they conjure up for you a richness of sight and smell which made it seem, they will say, "like Paradise". Cowslips in their hundreds sheeted the sloping meadows, bee and butterfly orchids stood thick in the damper fields in early summer. Huge scabious grew in the hedgerows and the high uplands behind Mr Clark's small holding were covered in heather, as his bees no doubt discovered. Up by Summerhouse Wood and in Mr. Down's fields in top Failand the tiny wild pansy, heartsease, was common. A few lone survivors of this little flower could still be found growing on the high ground by Summerhouse as late as the 1960s. White violets, again of great size, grew all along the banks beside the lanes and massed on the wide verges outside Failand House. In secret places, the wild daffodil flourished. The Frys, who never minded anyone enjoying their woodlands provided they did no damage, erected a notice down near Durbin's Batch which read:—

> 'All are welcome here. Do not
> disturb the birds nor pick the
> flowers greedily. Fair is the
> earth and goodly our heritage'.

Mushrooms in early autumn were so prolific that they were gathered by the laundry basketful in the misty fields, and sold in the city. The whole valley from Jubbes Court down to Portbury was splendid with apple blossom in its season. The cider apple orchards were planted by the Brown family who once lived in Jubbes Court and who founded the well-known Bristol firm of seed merchants. The last of these trees, now nearly a hundred years old, are blowing down one by one in the winter gales, their shallow roots no longer able to support the vast top hamper of branches but giving excellent cooking apples to the last. The white blaze of hawthorn bushes, once a striking sight, must have diminished, but the blossoming bushes are still about.

Before the chemicals, airborne from Avonmouth or sprayed by local farmers, put paid to the beautiful abundance and variety of wild flowers, and before the tractor replaced the horse drawn plough, Failand seemed to those who knew it then a little miracle, standing secluded, secure and unchanging within sight of the belching chimneys of Severnside. When the

Fry family made their gift to the National Trust of four hundred acres of their Failand estate one writer, a journalist named Charlie Thomas, wrote a piece for his newspaper, the *Evening Post*, in terms of such extravagance that he felt the need to explain why he held the little hamlet in such great affection. He wrote, he said, "like a lover. I am a lover and a part of my beloved country is safe for all time from the hand of the 'improver' and 'developer'". His language is the language of the journalist but his devotion rings true. "There is much more that I might say about this piece of England — the azure mist of bluebell time, the sweet smell of moss and primroses, and as now, the brave array of autumn; John Waite, the keeper, coming through the wood with the beaters; Isaac (Hardwick) ploughing Summerhouse with two great black horses; the sky reflecting blue on the brown furrows; children's laughter in the woods, and the great clouds like galleons in the sky, with the lark shaking down his melody."

There was one yearly celebration unique to Failand which seems to belong to simpler, happier times, and which serves exactly to people the lovely countryside of those pre-war years. This was the Chapel Tea. The Wesleyan chapel did not close until 1962 but it was in its heyday in the 1930s and we have plenty of first hand memories of the splendid occasion, always held on Good Friday. This mournful and solemn day in the church's calendar is not usually celebrated with feasting and merriment, but so it was in Failand, and what a success it was. They came from far and wide, not only chapel goers but anyone else who could manage to get in, including many who walked up from Pill, where they knew a good thing when they saw it. At its peak of popularity the Good Friday Tea required three sittings. All day Thursday local ladies baked great slabs of seed cake and cherry cake, using eggs from their own fowls; hot cross buns were sent out from Bristol; urns of tea were brewed with water from the well in the Tynings, since the lady in the cottage next to the chapel did not feel able, perhaps on religious grounds, to provide water from her tap. The fun and fellowship of this great occasion still echoes in the conversation of those who remember it. "It didn't seem like Good Friday when Chapel went." As surely as the cowslips and orchids have disappeared, so have such wholehearted simple pleasures, the full enjoyment of the moment as it passed instead of an anxious peering into the future. The least one may do is to record their passing.

Failand in Wartime (1939-44)

Failand, so near and yet so far from the bombs which fell continuously upon the city, must have seemed to Bristolians a blessed haven of peace. All kinds of people walked or cycled out there on summer days, or rode out on horseback, to sit in the garden of Manor Farm and enjoy their country tea, perhaps with the enormous treat added of a new laid egg or some cream. The farmer here took paying guests; one lady still living in Upper Failand stayed at the farm under this arrangement for a year, from 1940 to 1941. She had remembered having her tea in the garden there in earlier, quieter times and it seemed sensible if you were working in Bristol at least to sleep in comparative safety. Manor Farm, like many others during the war, was woefully short of able bodied help, and on one occasion a party of performers from the Bristol Hippodrome came out and lent a hand with the haymaking.

For part of the war there was a Prisoner-of-war camp in the fields opposite the Sixty Acre development. The vicar of Failand Church at that time, a man of compassion and good sense, the Rev. Bromhead, put it to his congregation from the pulpit one Sunday that they should take one of the German prisoners into their homes on Christmas Day. Many people did this, and in some cases formed friendships with their guests. In a house not far from Failand there still hangs an oil-painting, not an expert bit of work but reflecting in the intensity of its loving detail an exile's longing for home. This was painted in the camp by one of the P.O.W.s and given as a present to the Failand family who struck up a close relationship with him and his friends. The steep wooded hills, the wooden houses and the small church belong to some corner of Southern Germany or Austria. Almost all the picture is in shadow; the sun's rays light up only the very tops of the distant mountains. Anyone who has observed this lovely effect of the sunshine in the late afternoon in mountainous country will understand why the prisoner-artist kept it fresh in his imagination. How he must have longed to see it again.

After the war began Failand School had opened its doors to two schools from the London area. Barking and West Ham. The city children, as well as some from Bristol who came out to the safety of Failand to stay with relatives, dramatically increased the numbers at the little school. The Lower Hall opposite the church was taken into use as an extra classroom. The master in charge of the Londoners is still remembered, "a true

Cockney wit and a great morale booster. He and his family were billetted in Wraxall. He walked up to the school every morning, passing our building at about 10.00am with a cheery greeting". So writes Miss Frances Poole, who remembers him well. The school windows were covered with wire netting, and during the air-raids over Bristol, the children set on the floor and sang songs in their loudest voices when the gunfire was heavy. The West Ham contingent, who were taught in the Hall, moved across to the church for cover when the raids were on, and whiled away the time playing shove ha'penny on a board which they laid on top of the font!

One dreadful, exciting day a German plane, a Heinkel, circled overhead, obviously in trouble. The crew were seen to bale out, and with no-one in control the plane careered wildly about over Failand. All the schoolchildren, according to practice, were told to sit on the floor round the edge of the room. Suddenly a cleaner ran in from the schoolhouse next door. "It's all right," she shouted, rather inaccurately, "come out and see!" Everyone rushed out, regardless of danger, to see a parachute descending into the field by the church (the other pilot landed safely a little way off in Lord Wraxall's wood). Mr. Smith, the London schoolmaster, and another Mr. Smith, chauffeur at Failand House, approached the pilot who put up his hands — they must have had a gun — and refused a proffered cigarette. With a great politeness he then handed Mr. Smith, from West Ham, his beautiful leather airman's gloves as a souvenir. All this time the plane was in the sky above; it could have fallen anywhere and done real damage, but by the greatest good fortune it came to rest in a field behind Failand House, scattering its bombs as it fell. The school ran en bloc up the lane to see the wreck. By this time the whole hamlet was full of the army, the police and the fire brigade. At last when the excitement had died down everyone gathered again by the school. At this point it is well remembered that an officer of the Local Defence Volunteers, who must be nameless but who was renowned for never being on the spot when wanted, came hastily and alone down the road towards the school, his gun over his shoulder. "Where is he, Miss Poole?" But the courteous pilot, escorted away to a prisoner-of-war camp, was long gone.

Long before the war ended most of the evacuees had gradually drifted back to their parents in London, though a few stayed on and eventually settled down in the area. Failand School flourished for another forty years, for many of them under the marvellous headship of Miss Dorothy Cooke. The threat of closure hung over it like a small black cloud, for it was awkwardly situated in relation to the new predominant development of new houses in Upper Failand, and its buildings grew more and more out of date. The little school kept till the end its sturdy, old fashioned regard for the basic requirements of a sound education. By 1985 it could hold out no longer against the changing pattern of education. It closed at last, not with a whimper but a splendid bang. A great party, at which pupils from long ago mingled with the last children to learn in the old building, was followed by a service in Failand church. With enormous dignity and courage Miss Cooke, now retired and by this time a dying woman, waved away the offer of an arm to lean on and walked unaided down the long aisle to the front of the church to lead her old school in its last united act of worship. It is perhaps a blessing that she did not live long enough to watch the steady deterioration of the little Victorian building in which she and her colleagues had worked so long and so lovingly for the children of the hamlet.

Endpiece

One gloomy wet November afternoon some twenty years after the War ended, my daughter and I left the main Clevedon Road as it runs through Failand and turned our car down Oxhouse Lane. We were looking for a Victorian stone cottage described for us by the estate agent in rich prose, "a lovely house in an enchanting setting". As we got further and further from civilisation the mud increased and the strong smell of cow manure with it. The deep winding lanes seemed endless; when we finally saw Stone Cottage looming out of the fog our spirits were very low. We drove slowly past the plain front of the house as it abutted on to the road and tried to see in. Creepers and climbing shrubs run riot made this difficult, though we had a glimpse of a woman moving about in a front room. My daughter, then aged seven, told me emphatically that we could not possibly live out there "all on our own" among the endless dripping fields and hedges, and I was inclined to agree with her.

Another day, bright and clear, produced a different and lasting impression. We returned with an appointment, went inside, loved what we saw and came to settle. The house had been made by knocking two cottages into one just after the Second World War. There are two very similar ones in the neighbourhood, all built in the pinkish-brown stone of the district; several cottages were often put up at the same time for convenience sake, the same mortar mill serving all the buildings when the walls were constructed. They date from the eighteen seventies. The first of our pair had once been the home of the Emerys with whom the reader is already aquainted. We had not heard the last of this family, for ten years or so after we had bought our house a car drew up on a Sunday afternoon and an elderly lady came to our door. She was the Emerys' granddaughter. She had stayed in their cottage many times and was fascinated to walk in and visit it again. She had some photographs with her one of which she generously gave to us. In it George and Sarah with their daughter and grandson are standing at their front gate. The picture shows clearly how the front doors of the two houses were positioned at that time, fronting on the road (our front door is now round the side) and opening straight onto the steep staircases, one of which is still our way upstairs. There are holland blinds at the window of the front room and the window ledge inside is crowded with tall geraniums reaching for the light, an aspidistra and some large conch shells. More shells decorate the window ledge outside. I still keep shells in my front garden; the real change is that the flat road surface then ran right up to the base of the wall. Our grass bank is plainly the accumulation of the intervening years.

All we know of the other cottage is that it was once lived in by a tiny little woman, so small and frail that as she was out walking one day a great wind lifted her up and set her down in a holly hedge at the top of Failand Lane. There she was seen and picked out none the worse by the baker, Mr. Gerrish, who used to come up from Pill in a pony trap and his father before him, to deliver bread. Her house was called Rose Cottage. When we first came to Failand an old climbing rose called the Rambling Rector covered the whole of the front of the building — stems still spring green from the thick old roots and give a few flowers. We often dig up pieces of clay pipe on the Rose Cottage side of the garden so perhaps the little lady's husband smoked as he dug the vegetables. The earth in the top strip of what is still our vegetable garden patch is very dark, rich and crumbly, the end product of long cultivation, quite a different colour and texture from the lower section much more recently turned up.

And what of Failand now, late on in the twentieth century? The triangle of Sixty Acres in Upper Failand is now completely covered with houses. A few of the original bungalows built soon after the First World War remain among the newer properties. Once you turn down Oxhouse Lane into Lower Failand things are outwardly unchanged from earlier times but changes there are. Failand House where the Frys lived is, after many adventures, still a dignified private dwelling, now divided into several separate homes. Failand Hill House keeps its quiet beauty. The school and schoolhouse, closed in 1985, are so far empty and neglected, to the distress of those in the neighbourhood who remember the old buildings full of life and laughter.

Because of its nearness to Bristol our hamlet will always attract people here from the city to live among its green fields. It is the real country people though, the families whose names first began to appear in the church register long years ago, who give the place its character. I like to remember this when I stand in my garden on a clear night. On one side through the network of old apple branches I can see the reddish glow from the lights of the town. On the other the oaks, the hollies and the ash saplings are outlined against a country sky, their roots in the bank which marks the last remains of the Wansdyke.

Books consulted

Local pamphlets.
Findings of Failand.   Lucy Bowden.
Further Findings of Failand.   Lucy Bowden.
A Short History of Portbury.   W.J.R.
History of Wraxall.   Rev. Masters.
The Tale of Gordano.   Eve Wigan. Chatford House Press Ltd.
The Mystery of Wansdyke.   Albany Major and others.
Britain and Ireland in Early Christian Times.   Charles Thomas.
Roman Britain and the English Settlements.   Collingwood and Myers. O.U.P.
Lives of the Berkeleys.   John Smyth.
Memoirs of Sir Edward Fry.   Agnes Fry.
Margery Fry.   Enid Huw Jones.
Isabel Fry.   Beatrice Curtis Brown.
Roger Fry.   Virginia Woolf.

The Course of Wansdyke through Lower Failand

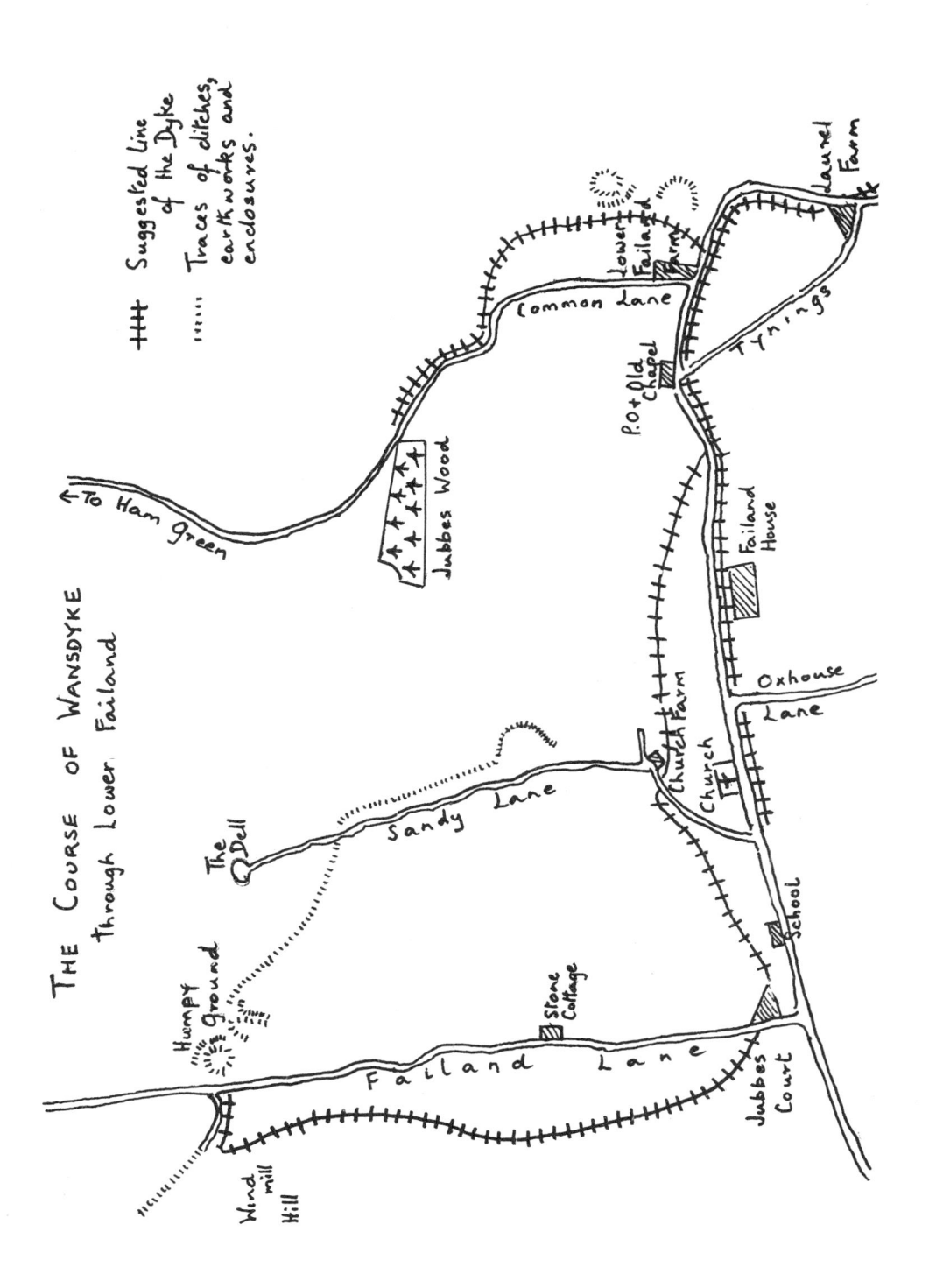

┼┼┼ Suggested line of the Dyke

······ Traces of ditches, earthworks and enclosures.

← To Ham Green

Jubbes Wood

Common Lane

Lower Failand Farm

Laurel Farm

Tynings

P.O. + Old Chapel

Failand House

Oxhouse Lane

Church Farm

Church

School

The Dell

Sandy Lane

Humpy Ground

Stone Cottage

Failand Lane

Jubbes Court

Wind mill Hill

Sketch Map of Lower Failand and neighbourhood.

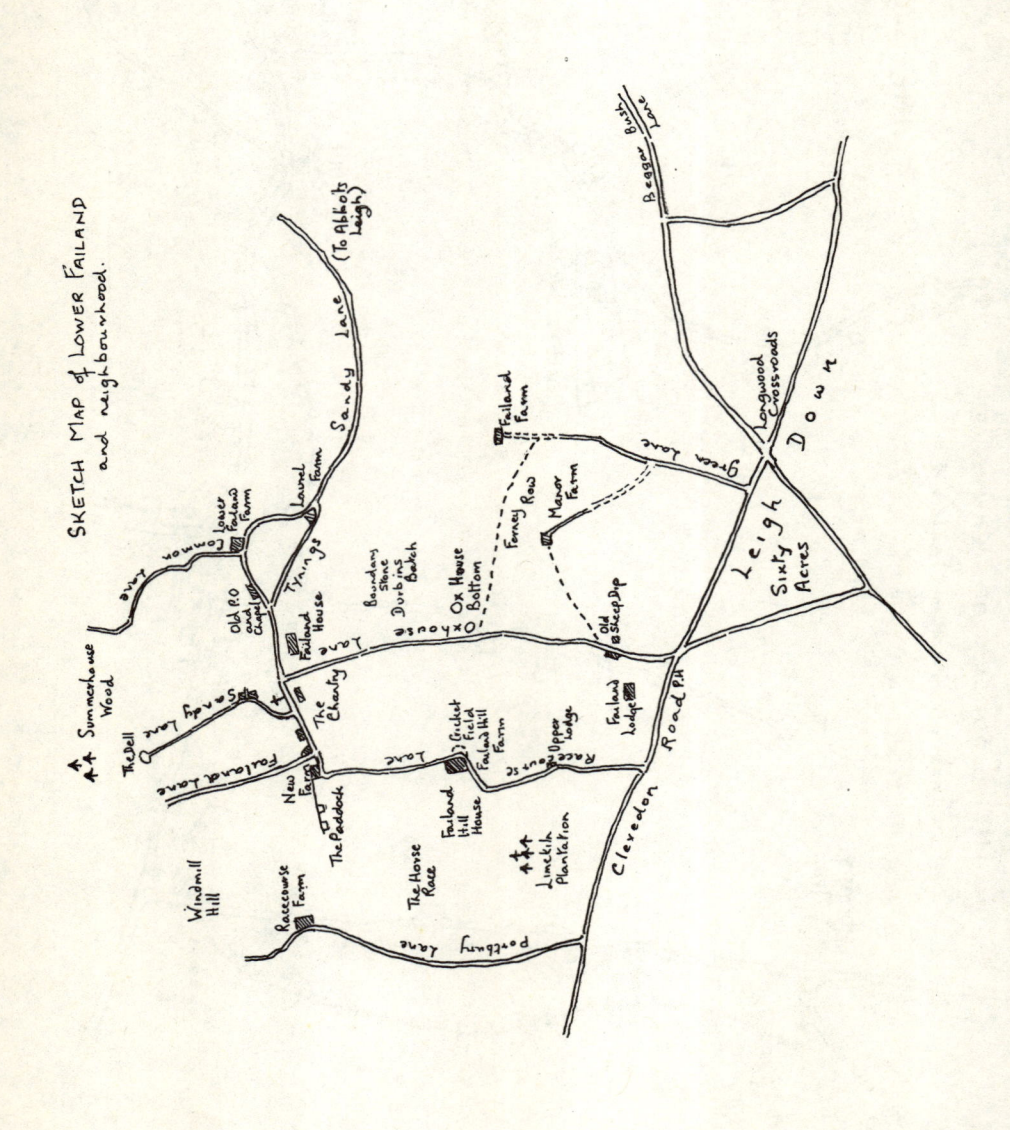